The False Houses

Edith Aron

The False Houses
Edith Aron

Paperback Edition First Published in the United Kingdom
in 2017 by aSys Publishing

eBook Edition First Published in the United Kingdom
in 2017 by aSys Publishing

Disclaimer

This is a work of fiction. Names, characters, businesses, places,
events and incidents are either the products of the author's
imagination or used in a fictitious manner. Any resemblance to
actual persons, living or dead, or actual events is
purely coincidental.

ISBN: 978-1-910757-88-8

aSys Publishing
http://www.asys-publishing.co.uk

*Translated by Rachel Isserlis and
Barbara Lester*

Contents

The False Houses

On the harbour front of Buenos Aires is a row of large, prominent wooden houses. From far away they look like fortresses or baroque edifices. With every visit and even after many years had passed, these houses always made a special impression on me – more and more. There was something fairy-tale-like about them, something unreal in this rather new country and perhaps that is why they were so fascinating.

On one occasion I wanted to examine them more closely and it was then I noticed that they weren't houses at all, but only seemed to be houses from the distance. They were actually vast wooden sheds – rather like London's Docklands, but in Buenos Aires.

Even now after many, many years, during any long journey (even those that were not as long as that to distant Buenos Aires), these remote, deceptive houses would resurface in her mind whenever she realised that she had made a grave error or had been mistaken in certain existential matters. Even in those places where she had imagined herself to be at home, she realised that she had been merely instrumental in the lives of others.

Time and time again during her life, filled with new hope, she had stumbled upon such false houses, until at last she understood that there was only one home for her, one that consisted of her memories and of *any* place where she had settled down – in whichever country, in whichever city.

Another way of doing it

Every Sunday morning since she had been living alone here in her London flat, she watched 'Breakfast with Frost' on BBC1. At precisely half past nine Frost marches across the stage, accompanied by a typical signature tune. In the background can be seen some features of large cities. Then he approaches the front of the screen, sits down and says: 'Welcome to this hour with Frost. Good morning!' He rubs his hands and introduces his programme. First of all the Sunday morning newspapers are presented, with commentaries by two specially invited prominent people. They talk about articles which they found particularly interesting and consider worthy of discussion. Then comes the announcement of the latest world news. One particularly popular announcer is Moira Stuart, who looks as if she, or at least her parents, must originally have come from the West Indies. It seems that viewers gradually tend to develop a preference for announcers that they observe on television getting older day by day, year by year. David Frost is an interviewer of the highest calibre and he tries to conduct these Sunday morning programmes in the most friendly and charming manner possible.

Last Sunday, in honour of the seventieth birthday of Mrs. Thatcher – which was celebrated everywhere with much ado – he showed part of an earlier interview with her.

That afternoon my 86-year-old neighbour, Ilse Wolff (who

had previously lived in Berlin) told me that she had been invited to Switzerland by friends to celebrate the 70th birthday of a friend. I didn't reply but I silently thought: 'And what shall I do to celebrate mine?'

After pondering a lot of different ideas, my daughter and I decided on a journey to Israel. I had always wanted to go there, although ideally first to Venice and to Greece, a city and a country which I had not yet visited. We went to the offices of the El Al airline on Regent Street where we bought air tickets and reserved four nights in the cheapest hotel we could find in the brochure for Tel Aviv.

We flew from London Heathrow. The security was extremely strict. The aeroplane was full of young people in blue shirts, on their way to various kibbutzim. In the middle of the plane was a large screen on which were shown landscapes connected with the Old Testament. There were generous portions of tasty food. One could pick one's own newspaper or wait for the papers to be handed out. I chose the Jerusalem Post and saw that on the following evening there was to be a peace gathering at Kikar Malkei Yisrael Square with a speech by Amos Oz. "We'll go there tomorrow!" I said to my daughter. When the plane landed at four in the morning at Ben Gurion airport, the blue-shirted Boy Scouts clapped and cheered. The airport was practically empty at this early hour. We changed money and took a taxi to the hotel in Ness-Ziona Street which is very near the promenade and the beach. Rather strange, these first impressions – the tropical landscape, the palm trees, the modern buildings lining the beach. It was a young country which reminded me of parts of South America – Brazil for instance.

The next morning, we went first of all to the sea, strolled along the promenade and admired the many elegant hotels, including the Hilton. Then we found a route through the town which led us to the old market quarter. We were struck by all the busy to-ing and fro-ing of the people, the shouting, the peddling of wares and the general commotion. We looked at lots of things but hardly bought anything. Every now and then we sat on the terrace of a café and had a cool drink. It was already late Friday afternoon. We heard people wishing each other a 'Good Sabbath' – the only words we could understand – for the next day was Saturday, the great day of rest in Israel, Sunday being the equivalent of Monday in the Christian world.

In the evening we were seated in a restaurant on the promenade. Every now and then we could make out the sounds of South American music. After we had finished our dinner, we wandered in the direction of the music and came upon a crowd of people. In the middle stood four Bolivian musicians, animatedly playing their instruments. The group was called 'Bolivia canta' and, despite the warm evening, the musicians stood draped in their ponchos and were wearing hats. We joined the crowd, listened, clapped to the beat and soon got talking to the others. Among them was a Chilean who had settled there. He was doing well. ("Soy christiano," he said, "pero aqui me quedo" – 'I'm Christian, but I'll stay here.') A woman from Venezuela joined the conversation – she was on a visit with her father and staying in one of the luxury hotels opposite. After a while the Bolivians had a break and, hearing the Spanish language, joined in. They liked it there too; they had a decent flat, lots of work and had made some recordings. Immediately they offered to sell us their cassettes.

"And these ponchos, aren't they too hot for this climate?" I asked.

"Of course, but they're part of the atmosphere of our work."

In the meantime it was twenty to midnight. Soon was to be the big, important birthday, respected and specially celebrated everywhere in the world. ???My daughter went away for a moment, saying she would be back in a second. She disappeared into the restaurant opposite. After a while she came back with a package in her hand and whispered something to the Bolivians. She handed out some cardboard plates, plastic forks and paper cups which had been in the package. And then it was midnight.

The Bolivians stood one behind the other in line with their

guitars and panpipes, singing 'Happy Birthday to You' in Spanish and English. The listeners clapped. Someone became quite emotional. An elegant, thin, long red candle was lit, chocolate was offered around and drinks were poured into the paper cups.

"We've never played this song outside on the street before." said one musician.

"And I've never been to a street birthday party before." said another.

"Unfortunately, I can't tell you how old I am today, otherwise you'd all fall flat on your backs!" They all laughed and, of course, they wanted to know how old I was – but they never found out.

The next day we turned right out of Ness-Ziona Street, up the hill past a Hungarian restaurant. We were on our way to find a German bookshop. We'd heard that the owner of this bookshop often used to dine with Max Brod at the Hungarian restaurant. We turned into Ben-Yehuda Street and there was the German bookshop on the corner. A certain Frau Parnes had taken over the shop after the death of her husband. Many books by Joseph Roth were exhibited in the shop window. It was Saturday morning but nevertheless the shop was open – or at least, the door was open. We went in straightaway and immediately noticed a poster with the words 'We supply books for the Goethe Institute.' An elderly woman sat at a writing table; next to her stood a young man.

"We're only here by chance," said the young man. "Today is Saturday and normally all the shops are closed."

"Alright, then we'll come back tomorrow." we said.

We looked for a restaurant where one could have a good lunch; however, we didn't find anything that really appealed to us. In the end we landed up in the restaurant of an elegant hotel overlooking the sea. When a diner wanted to light a cigarette after his meal, he was immediately told by a waiter: "It is forbidden to smoke here on the Sabbath."

"That's all we need!" we thought to ourselves.

We spent the afternoon at the beach and towards evening we went to Kikar Malkei Yisrael Square with its great bronze

Holocaust memorial (it was the square where, two years and two months later, on the 4th November 1995, Jitzak Rabin was to be murdered.) The speaker on this particular evening was Amos Oz. Unfortunately we couldn't understand a single word of Hebrew but luckily we discovered that, just by chance, the young man whom we'd met that morning in the German bookshop was standing right next to us. He was very friendly, translating the speech for us into English and also partly into German. His parents came from Hamburg and Berlin. Later on he offered to show us a bit of Tel Aviv and drove us in his car right up to Jaffa, where we ate dinner next to the sea at the Benny Haday'ag (Benny the Fisherman) restaurant

"My mother is … years old today."

"Well, well." said the young man, "My mother is exactly the same age." He told us about the antique section of the bookshop run by a Herr Laske.

After four days, as planned, we drove to Jerusalem. On entering the city, it was beautiful to see all the white stone buildings spread out over several hills. We thought about Else Lasker-Schüler, who is buried at the foot of the Mount of Olives and also Paul Celan, who had visited Israel in the last year of his life. We drove up to Massada and bathed in the Dead Sea, marvelling at the landscape of this old-new country.

Just before leaving Israel, we drove to Tel Aviv. There I met old schoolfriends from the town in Saarland where I was born, who had emigrated to Israel in 1937. Now they were Israelis (or rather had remained 'Hebrews') but still spoke perfect German. That was a great joy. Walter still had sticking-out ears. That's how I recognised him.

Despite everything, I suddenly wanted to see some German books and so I visited the Goethe Institute. Downstairs in the entrance hall, I noticed a sculpture. It was by the American sculptor, Bernhard Reder. The subject was a girl playing 'cat's cradle'. This game is usually played by schoolgirls, winding a length of yarn over both little fingers. I was reminded of a train journey from Paris to Berlin, a long, long time ago; opposite me sat a girl, about eight years old, who invited me to play cat's cradle with her. We played for nearly an hour until she had to change trains in Hanover.

The House in Nahuel Huapi Street

I now want to talk about the house in Nahuel Huapi Street, the house very close to Coghlan, a suburban station. When sitting at the breakfast table we could hear the train bells ringing, announcing either the arrival from Retiro or the departure to Tigre. Both are suburbs of Buenos Aires and also termini of the city's train line. But perhaps those trains also went to Borges, a station named after an ex-general, the grandfather of Jorge Luis Borges.

I moved in with my friend after my mother and I had lost our apartment and I, with a wardrobe, a bed, a mattress and a small bookcase, needed to find new accommodation. The idea was that I would only need it for three weeks, but in the end this became a year.

In this house you always had to turn up for mealtimes on the dot. Anyone who could not manage that had to telephone and let them know, and in other ways, too, the house rules had to be strictly observed. At home at my mother's that sort of thing was not taken that seriously and there was an altogether freer atmosphere. Here, it was not really a proper kind of family life; but this new house was large and roomy and on two floors. On the ground-floor were the sitting-room and the dining-room. In the sitting-room there stood an old-fashioned dark bookcase and a piano. Whenever you wanted to see the books you had to open the glass door which was hidden behind a dark-blue curtain. I cannot recollect the titles of the books, but maybe I never looked at them properly anyway. In one corner there was also a big grand-father clock. Every time I looked at the clock and listened to its chimes, I thought of my father in France, far away on another continent, and of a funny thing he had said about the grandfather clock in our own house: "If you sit here for an hour and call out after every chime 'He goes here, he goes there' then you'll get five Francs." At that time, before the referendum, we had lived in the Saar region. If I fell in with his suggestion he instantly reconsidered and promised "If you keep quiet and stop doing this, you'll get the money anyway."

Having told this episode, I then also always remembered the falling-down story. If my father was walking twenty paces ahead in the road and I happened to fall over he called out: "Come over here and I'll help you get up again." Of course, I did just that and realized much too late that he had once again played a trick on me. And then there was the matter of the jar of mustard which worked out in much the same way as the one concerning the grandfather clock pendulum: at first I was promised five Francs were I to eat all the mustard, but when I had hardly begun, I got the money to make me stop.

In the big sitting-room in Nahuel Huapi Street there was also a desk with a portrait of my friend's father on top. Gerd, the eldest son, who was at art school, had painted it. Also in the room was a little round table which was never without a table-cloth, nor without a vase with fresh flowers from the garden placed exactly in the middle. Around the table there were two or three comfort-able armchairs as well as the world's most comfortable sofa. At least that is what I thought at the time. I sat on that sofa hour after hour, sometimes through entire nights, staring at the grand-father clock. It seems that even then I already knew that later on in life I would remember this room and those empty hours that I allowed to pass by. Sometimes I did listen to music, though, since at my mother's we had neither a radio nor a record player. Thus I discovered Chopin's piano concertos, listened to the Capriccio Espanol and Sheherazade by Rimsky-Korsakov, French songs sung by Maurice Chevalier, or perhaps by Mistinguett, and then all the fabulous old Argentinian tangos from the 1930s such as 'Yira, Yira', 'Don Juan', 'La Morocha', 'El chocolo', 'A media luz', 'Rodriguez Pena'.

I admired the way my friend managed to run the house and to give orders although she was still so very young. Maria the cook and Valeria the maid obeyed her. Maria was the mother of 12 children. Whenever a letter from France arrived from my father she first hid it and only handed it over to me if I gave her something for her grandchildren; by now there were 16 of them. She assumed there would be money in the letters, and often that was indeed the case. Usually it was one of those lovely old blue 1000 Franc notes, and occasionally more than one of them.

On Sundays, Valeria, the chamber maid, spent hours in front of the mirror in order to dress stylishly. All that her outing amounted to was that she crossed the road to treat herself to an ice cream for a few centavos.

My friend never found out how often, in her absence, I had tried on her fur coat, her leather jacket, her smart suits and her elegant summer dresses. And sometimes, when I had a date in town with a young man and knew that she was going to go out herself, I wore her elegant clothes. Whenever she came home before me, I put away her things in the wardrobe in the hall upstairs, the wardrobe that I had brought with me; and next morning, while she was getting ready in the bathroom, I quickly transferred everything to her own cupboard, and ten minutes later she put on those same things without suspecting anything.

"Last night, seemingly in a dream, you cried out loudly, as you do often," she sometimes told me. She could not know how uneasy my little secrets made me feel. If only her things didn't fit me so well! On my meagre office salary I could never afford more than a skirt or a blouse, or maybe a winter coat on hire purchase.

At the big house and in the adjoining garden, grand fiestas or parties were frequently organized. Friends got together, brought along bottles of Sidra and danced the tango on the terrace. When all the guests had left and everybody in the house was asleep, the eldest brother and I stayed behind downstairs on the comfortable sofa. After a while we switched off the light, and in the morning at breakfast we hardly dared look each other in the eye. This was repeated every few weeks. Sometimes we actually arranged to meet at one o'clock in the morning, downstairs in the sitting-room. One time we heard a door open on the first floor. In a panic he ran off, in his haste taking my pyjamas with him. Startled, I hid behind the sofa. When the house had fallen silent again Gerd came back, and we burst out laughing, regretting at the same time that we couldn't tell anyone about all this.

Fairly soon after this the old father was taken ill; he died a few weeks later. Now the three siblings were all alone. I remember one Christmas there. We were sitting downstairs in the drawing-room, and the three clasped each other's hands. The younger brother Mino, pet name for Mario, took my hand, too. I was deeply touched. Six months after their father's death the two older ones celebrated a double engagement. The youngest brother went to live with his uncle. The house was sold. And therefore, at last, I joined my own father in France.

Finchley Road and the Swimming Pool

In my younger days, I once read the following in a book: 'One can live in solitude, but then the sun at least has to be your friend.' (Nietzsche). I don't know whether I am interpreting this sentence correctly, but anyway, right now the sun is shining, it is Sunday, and it is summer…I get ready to go out, pick up my swimming bag, which is always packed, walk down to the corner and wait for the 82 bus, a red English double-decker, to take me to North Finchley Terminus. Whenever I go up Finchley Road my eyes alight on Patterson Road, where the manager of the 'Pen Club of German Writers Abroad' used to live. Further along is the first significant stop 'Golders Green' (sic). Looking out of the window I spot Hodford Road and I remember that, as a little girl, my daughter went there for occasional ballet lessons. Directly opposite live Mr. Krysler and his wife. She was from Düsseldorf and he from Hesse, both having emigrated here in the 50s. Mr. Krysler, who is older than his wife, still identifies with German culture and looks after the public relations for the 'Club 43', which is rather like a German cultural association abroad. I once listened to a reading there by Erich Fried. He was reading something about the former East Germany, and about the early years of his exile here.

I first heard this club mentioned by the historian J.W. Bruegel, born in Brno, who was giving a lecture on the Hitler-Stalin-Pact. That was in 1986. I had met him and his wife at the Karl Kraus Symposium at the Institute of Germanic Studies. Earlier on in Vienna he had looked after the estate of Karl Kraus. Four days after that lecture he died unexpectedly. He was a charming, lively, very elderly gentleman. Every day he read the 'Neue Zürcher Zeitung'. It struck me that quite a few German emigrés did likewise. England unintentionally became yet another exile for me. The fourth one. Life in the Paris years had been quite different; I had not perceived them as exile.

I thought about all that when sitting on the bus as it was making its way up the Finchley Road. One had to get off the bus at the next stop to the left if one wanted to visit the expressionist poetess Henriette Hardenberg, who was still alive at the time. Now one has to get off one stop earlier, opposite the Hotel Central, then walk up Hoop Lane for a few hundred metres, with the entrance to Golders Green Crematorium to your right, where she found her last resting-place. It is a big beautiful park with many flowers and wall plaques, or commemorative panels placed there by families and friends. To name but a few from the index of celebrities who are buried there: TS Eliot, Alexander Fleming, Sigmund Freud, Julian Huxley, Rudyard Kipling, Vivian Leigh, Anna Pavlova, Ronnie Scott, Peter Sellers, George Bernard Shaw, H.G. Wells.

The bus rolled on; you see something like a large meadow where horses and cows are grazing, and sometimes even a sheep or two. Every time I ask myself why, so unexpectedly and in the middle of town, there is suddenly a piece of land on which animals can graze.

But before that, there is a great big junction where buses and cars turn left into Hendon Way and then on to Brent Cross with its huge American-style shopping mall. To the right, road signs point in the direction of Tilbury Port where ages ago we had disembarked from our ocean liner. Also on this corner, there is a pub where in summer one can enjoy sitting outside. In the garden, the statue of a golden eagle serves as an ornament, and that is also the name of the pub: 'The Golden Eagle'. Nowadays the ashes of a man, who had loved this pub and had first shown it to us, lie in an ornamental lake in another beautiful park, a park in which there are no commemorative plaques, a park near Baker Street which is open to the general public, at a spot at which there is a little wooden bridge and also, strangely, just such an eagle statue. He, too, had loved this park and had been the one to show it to us first. The bus continues on its way, following the Finchley Road, until it gets to Finchley Central. There one sees many young people wearing the typical little Oriental caps; there are restaurants and shops, all selling salt beef and latkes – in effect pickled meat and potato cakes – and a gherkin, should you wish to have one. You are now in the Finchley constituency where Mrs. Thatcher began her political career in 1959.

Nearby is the terminus for the No. 82 bus which, from the stop at my street corner, next to the house with the blue plaque where Oskar Kokoschka had lived until 1980, goes all the way to North Finchley terminus. There you can change to the 263 bus and continue for a further two stops to the North Finchley Open Air Swimming Pool. 1-2-3-4 bus, 6-7-8-9 bus, 11-12-13-14 bus, 16-17-18-19 bus. That is an English children's game. Instead of 5-10-15-20 etc. you have to say 'bus'. Whenever you get it wrong it's the next person's turn. I played all these games with my little daughter in all the years I took her swimming. Or another game: I spy with my little eye something beginning with 'B'. You then have to think of a noun describing something you can see out in the street, or wherever. If you guess correctly, it is then your turn, otherwise the other person continues. At that time we went down the High Road and in a Pakistani-owned shop bought either an ice cream, a drink or those tiny round, pink and white, sweet-and-sour boiled sweets which were my daughter's particular favourites. A few steps further along we stopped outside a garage and, fascinated, watched huge, long , coloured brushes automatically wash cars from all sides, as the cars were being lifted by a big, flat, open panel. At the time this way of doing things was very new. Sometimes the brushes were red, sometimes green or blue. In one of his films Eric Rohmer also draws our attention to this method of car-washing. All this happened many years ago. The garage no longer exists, but the Pakistani's little shop is still there.

There was another shop, also no longer there, where I bought a lovely old used copy from 1840 of the 'Pickwick Papers', Charles Dickens's first novel, published when he was only 25. The paper is very thin, and there are 928 pages. The cover is made of fine dark green leather, and on the spine, in golden letters, is printed the name Charles Dickens and the title of the book, plus the kind of pretty ornamentation in fashion at the time.

I once saw a similar edition in Paris, at Paul Celan's. I liked it so much that he spontaneously gave it to me as a present. (He was spontaneous, always.) Perhaps he, too, had acquired it here in London. Or in Paris at the 'Bookinistes'. Strangely enough, it was a book by Carlyle. I think the cover sported a small golden owl.

I had been going to this pool for a number of years. Some of the faces I recognized year after year. There was the Hungarian doctor who had been living and practising here for years, still very much the European, always swimming in the butterfly style, always greeting people from afar in a friendly but reserved manner, and usually uttering the same sentence: "How is your daughter?"

I replied: "She is fine, she is a big girl now and lives abroad." Once I told him that I had been to Vienna and Salzburg and, in Vienna, had seen a road sign with an arrow pointing in the direction of Budapest and that on my travels I always liked seeing such things. But this did not appear to be of any interest to him. He also never spoke German although he understood it pretty well. I once told him: "I have been coming here for at least 12 years." and he said: "And I for 18 years."

Another one was a strange Englishman with whom I

exchanged a few words now and again. The last thing I heard from him was: "I have sold my boat, my house is next, and after that, my car. I am going to move to Florida for 3 years. For tax reasons."

"To Miami?" I asked.

"Oh no, that is far too touristy for me. Somewhere near St. Petersburg. It is nice and quiet there, and the crime rate is very low. Only this morning my friends rang me and asked when on earth I would turn up. But first I'll have to sell my house and my car. If the house sale takes too long, I'll let it instead."

"I have to leave a bit earlier today," I said, "because I'm going to the opening of an exhibition here in London by the sister of a friend of mine who lives in Scotland."

"You live in St. Johns Wood, don't you?"

"Yes, opposite the EMI Studios in Abbey Road. On the Beatles record 'Abbey Road' there is a picture of the zebra crossing and of the house where I live."

"I have to go to that part of London right now. May I give you a lift home?"

Somewhat surprised, I said: "Yes please – why not, but only if you are going there anyway."

"It's on my way. I'll change quickly now and meet you at the exit in 5 minutes."

"No." I said, "In about 12 minutes. I don't like rushing unless absolutely necessary."

"Alright then," he said, "see you shortly."

12 minutes later I turned up at the exit. He had a very smart and comfortable car. He was about to turn on the radio full blast, but he must have sensed that I wasn't impressed by that. He drove through some side streets. Everywhere was very leafy, and this summery London was truly beautiful. There was little traffic.

"I am now going to my Golf Club," he said. "In Hendon."

"But doesn't that mean you have to go back?" I enquired.

"No big deal by car," he claimed.

In no time we found ourselves in Abbey Road and outside my

house. When I tried to bid him farewell and to thank him, my 'taxi driver' unexpectedly told me that his name was Paul and that he would like to ask a favour.

"Well?" I said, much surprised. Would it be possible for him to change quickly at my place since otherwise he would be denied entry to his club.

"Bien oblige," I thought, and reluctantly said yes. I told him the number of my flat and went ahead, while he went to park the car somewhere. Before long he rang the bell, and there he was at my door. I showed him to the bathroom so he could change, but he did not seem to like that. So I let him use the big room and slammed the door. What on earth is he doing all that time, I asked myself after 5 minutes which seemed to me like an eternity. But then he did come out, reeking of perfume, and I said: "I can't offer you anything because I have to leave any minute now, as I already told you, to attend the opening of that exhibition. And it's quite late now."

"Yes, yes, I do understand," he said, whereupon I opened the front door.

"Thank you for allowing me to change my clothes here."

"And thank you for giving me a lift home," I said, closing the door with a big sigh of relief once he was outside. Why had this complete stranger been in my room, I wondered. All that was on the Thursday.

On Saturday I went swimming again. Luckily, the man called Paul who had seen part of my flat, and whom I didn't actually know, was nowhere to be seen. Perhaps he had already gone to America. But on the next day, Sunday, something quite unexpected happened. I had briefly entertained the idea of treating myself to a day at the seaside. It is never very far to the sea, 1½ or 2 hours, and before you know it, you're in Birchington-on-Sea, in Margate or Broadstairs, where you find Charles Dickens's 'Bleak House', named after the novel he is said to have written after his last stay there . But that summer I had not yet renewed my British Railcard, and it sometimes happened that, while one was sitting on the train the sun shone splendidly, and as soon as one got to the resort the sun had vanished and it had become very windy. That's why I set off once again for my usual swimming pool; within 45 minutes I could be in the water, and enjoy the sun. Thought turned into action. The pool was pretty crowded. One even had to queue for ages just to get a ticket. There were so many people there that even in the water there wasn't much room to swim. Then all of a sudden, there were no longer so many people in the water. They were standing around the edges. The steps that I always used to enter the water were blocked. Someone was dangling their feet in the water. Perhaps that was why so many people were standing at the side of the pool. I walked to the opposite end of the pool and jumped in. I swam and enjoyed the lovely sunny day. At the spot where the crowd had gathered and the feet were dangling in the water I saw half a torso which popped up again and again to a certain rhythm, rather like someone doing their exercises. I swam backwards and forwards, then climbed out of the water and asked somebody what was going on. I got no answer but was stared at angrily. The crowd drew closer and closer around this spot, and there was hardly anyone in the water any more. Next to me a young man was saying: "He'd have done better to have stayed at home today."

Then some policemen and an ambulance man appeared. The crowd standing to the right headed for the exit, as if they were providing an escort, and now the place with the steps could be seen, deserted. Two girls appeared carrying a large bucket of water and poured it, several times, across that spot, as if they were trying to wash away something that wasn't really dirty at all. This was repeated several times. Now the steps were being used once more, and the pool gradually filled up again with people. Everything had happened quietly, without any kind of suspicious or alarming noises. There were people around, though, who had not come to use the pool but were now approaching with their notepads, stopping to talk to various individuals and conducting what looked like interviews. Then a familiar face walked past. It turned out to be the BBC actor with whom a year earlier I had discussed the accident on the river Thames, in which one boat had collided with another one, leading to the sinking of the 'Marchioness'. My daughter, too, had lost friends who had been on that boat on that fateful evening.

"Do you know what happened here?"

"Didn't you see the stretcher? They carried away the man."

"No," I said, "I only saw the assembled crowd."

"The man is dead. He had jumped off the diving board into the water and somebody jumped after him too soon and is said to have fallen onto his head. The result was that he remained under water rather too long before he was noticed. They tried to revive him but couldn't help him anymore."

I now understood those movements made by the torso which I had spotted from the water, that had been bobbing up regularly. They said it had been a young man. He was one of the group that had been lying in the sun near me, one of whom had said: "He'd have done better to have stayed at home today."

This incident was to have serious repercussions for the pool management. The following summer ticket prices were exorbitantly increased, and only a limited number of swimmers were accepted.

By the next year the pool had been closed. All the doors and windows were nailed shut with wooden slats.

The next year, the whole place was demolished.

The Rabbits

Yesterday she visited some friends. Everything was harmonious and as it should be, until at the end they went to inspect his study. There, standing on the edge of a book shelf, were some miniature rabbits, carved from wood. She looked at them more closely and read that they had been imported from Italy. "How charming!" she cried and very carefully picked up one of them in order to look at it and admire it properly from all sides. He stood next to her and now they both looked at these delicate, tiny wooden rabbits and laughed together. He suddenly called out in a loud voice: "Miranda!" At once his wife came running down the stairs.

"There is someone here who likes your rabbits. You can have them as a present," he said, "But remember the story 'Letter to a young lady in Paris'." he added, laughing somewhat feebly and yet wagging his index finger as if conveying a warning at the same time; and then he handed her a small box with the six rabbits in it. Again they all laughed. However, something began to gnaw inside her. Why did he mention that story? As soon as she got home, she went to find the book and re-read the story. It told of someone who was living in a borrowed flat and, without any kind of rational explanation, began to vomit rabbits. Every day there were more and more and they not only ruined the flat but destroyed him, too.

Suddenly she no longer wanted the rabbits, however cute they were. She didn't want to throw them away either, and just to pass them on to somebody else also seemed the wrong thing to do. So, with her apologies, she returned the dainty present. She herself would be going to Italy soon and she would be able to buy these same miniature rabbits for herself.

Things that happened in the past should stay there.

If he did vomit them again, there was nothing she could do about it.

Au printemps tout est bon!

"Where does the name of this famous store come from, do you know who called it that?" piped up a voice among the thirty new employees who were sitting in the hall, being introduced to the traditions of this distinguished old department store in Paris.

"I can't answer that particular question – we don't know. The store was founded in 1865 and then it was expanded at regular intervals. New bits kept being added to it and, as you know, now it consists of two large buildings with a connecting bridge in the middle."

"I'm pleased that you have got a proper job at last," wrote her father from the border town in Lorraine. "Your grandmother's brother from Lixheim already worked there in 1895."

"The customers are like kings and queens," they were informed by the voice from the lectern at the front. "Never forget that. Always be courteous and never lose your patience. All that matters is that you make a sale."

During the three summer months, the scholarship, or student grant, did not get paid so Irene was happy to have found this work. Her four languages were useful here. She was sent to the hairdresser's, as her hair always had to look smart, and every day she had to wear her good, black suit. On the left lapel was the word 'Interpreter' with a list of her languages on a background of blue, red and white stripes. Her code signal was five little bell rings which could be heard in both houses. At that signal she had to go to the translators' central assembly point from where she got sent to various departments to help the customers make themselves understood. The boss was called Monsieur Laporte and the woman with the thick spectacles, sitting behind the writing desk, was Madame Alexandra. She had been working in this store for thirty years. Some of the employees had started work as liftboys at the age of fifteen or seventeen and were now nearly sixty-five years old; they stood around in their uniforms handing out leaflets with information about the week's special offers. Once retired, their pension was so meagre that they could hardly live off it. I am describing conditions here as they were years ago. I saw women who had been working in the belt department for over thirty years and were just waiting for the day when they could retire and move to the south, where sunshine was guaranteed and they could exist in poverty for another few years. Pretty, neat and respectable looking women sprayed one with scent in the perfume department. Many of them were unmarried mothers whose children were cared for at a home during the week. Others stood day in, day out, year after year, in the department where all kinds of scarves were sold along with the accompanying loops and clips, demonstrating how these could be used. Their movements and speech became completely mechanical. Had they retired, their pensions would have been so small that they would neither have been able to live, nor to die on them. They just had to cope until the end of their lives. Money was always scarce.

There were other new sales assistants as well as myself, including a Finnish student and also an elderly, conscientious and mature Swedish lady who was happy to be able to work in such an elegant shop at her advanced age.

Upstairs on the fifth floor were the dining rooms; on the right was the restaurant for the customers and, on the left, the staff canteen. Occasionally, when a customer wanted company, he invited one of the translators for a meal. There one learnt the art of comparison – although the food in the French staff canteen always tasted much better and there was more choice than in the canteens of other countries.

In the mornings, when there was not much happening, one could try on dresses, blouses and coats on the first floor if one so wished; and if we, the staff, wanted to buy something, we could of course do so much more cheaply and pay in monthly instalments – that is to say, it was taken off our monthly salaries. It was fun trying on all sorts of clothes. And we liked the music department. A Finnish student, Anni Wächter, and I had similar tastes. On another floor were the lovely fabrics, patterned, checked or plain, all beautifully laid out, each in its own place.

When I first started to work there I was always on the side of the customer – for instance, if someone tried on gloves for half an hour and then left without having decided on a pair, I would encourage them in this behaviour. Then the boss found out and said: "Your job is to convince the customers that they have to buy something. You are working for us, aren't you?"

Once, by coincidence on my birthday, an American came and bought a bidet. I steered him towards a comfortable one. "Is it to wash babies in or wash them out? You do know that joke, don't you," he said. "When country people saw bidets for the first time in a department store in a big city, the women asked this question quite innocently."

I did not know the joke but I laughed anyway. He gave me a generous tip.

On the same day, some Argentine friends of mine, who had been living in Italy for a year, turned up. They seemed to be rather worried about me and about how I was doing. I believe they invited me to dinner and also to the cinema and encouraged me to stay in touch with them. That is to say, with the man with whom I had been going out before he married the woman he had now brought with him to the store. And now they suddenly wanted to be really good friends with me. I suppose they meant well, in their own way.

The False Houses

I found myself once again in the wrong place. Why did I accept? Was I really so lost? Every time I went to their house (for they invited me there regularly) first of all I would lock myself in the bathroom and cry a bit. Then I went upstairs and sat down at the table. The man would look at me searchingly and the woman sometimes washed up the plates a bit too loudly and reminded me indiscreetly every now and then that the man had things to do and it was now time to go. I recognised the yellow and gold checked napkins which clearly remained from my time. (Once the man gave me a few sheets of paper to read, for he was writing a book, and asked me if I was interested in it. He had written, for example, 'I kissed your shoulders and played with the roses of your breasts' etc.)

One day, many years later, when he had been living abroad for some time, a thick book arrived by post with a cool and distant dedication: 'for Irene, who ...' His book became a worldwide success and he was proud of the central female character which was so convincing in a literary sense but of course had absolutely nothing to do with me.

Then once, amongst the customers, I recognised some friends of my mother's from Buenos Aires. Another time the singer Lena Horne came and bought some cheap antiques and on another occasion Juliette Greco sat, surrounded by lots of people, signing autographs and at the same time advertising some product or other. Presumably she was very well paid for that.

At nine o'clock every morning the doormen had to make their way to the various entrances. An interpreter was sent to each door. Background music resounded through the loudspeakers: the Swedish Rhapsody, which was a hit at the time. When we first started to work there, we had to wander around the store for a whole week, learning on which floor one could buy shoes, blouses, perfume and so on, so that one could always advise the customers – rather like taxi drivers who have to be tested on the whereabouts of all the streets, parks and squares in a big city.

During the first two weeks my colleagues and I (I mean the

ones who started to work there at the same time as me) noticed various tourists in the store every day from early in the morning, mostly wearing the same clothes with sunglasses and with cameras hanging on straps. It was only after a fortnight that we realised that these were house detectives to whom we had deliberately not been introduced since they were also keeping an eye on us, the new employees. After all, in a department store all the wares lie around openly. Their conversation went something like this: "Tu travailles aujourd'hui?" "C'est calme," answered the other, "Très calme." That meant that they had not caught anyone – to put it politely – 'borrowing'. If they did notice someone taking things without paying, they would not say anything at first but continued to observe that person. Then a secret bell code could be heard throughout the store and the person would be watched by all the store detectives. Shoplifters often start to feel safe and take more and more things. It is not until they want to leave that they feel a tap on their shoulder and at the same time, hear a shrill bell ringing. If the person immediately admits that the things are stolen and if he or she is prepared to pay for them, all is well and forgotten. But if they deny it, they are taken to another department and interrogated by the store police; if they continue to refuse to admit to the theft, they are handed over to the regular police and taken to court. Sometimes, if they happened to be foreigners, I would get called upon to translate.

"You shouldn't be so considerate and gentle," said the plain-clothes policeman to me. "First of all you have to make this woman cry and then after she has confessed to everything she pinched today, you have to insist that she bring back all the stuff she has accumulated at home. You'll be amazed."

Sure enough, the next day appeared bottles of perfume, costly lace, expensive lipsticks, elegant writing paper – all the things that she had appropriated over time. I had to speak German with the woman. She was a middle-aged Austrian, from Vienna.

Then one day it was a man from Uruguay, a tourist who was stealing sunglasses. To excuse himself he kept murmuring: "But

I'm Uruguayan, after all, I'm from Uruguay," and laid his passport on the table as though it could wash away his crime. He paid, and all was forgotten.

Next there was a stubborn Yugoslav who spoke German but kept denying everything and had already been held for two days. Together with the French store detective who had caught him, I had to go to the court on the Île de la Cité to help translate. Amongst other things the young man had stolen some valuable earrings; they were intended as a present for his sister. "Vous vouliez des souvenirs pas chers de Paris," said the judge, and everyone laughed. He had to go to prison for he had no money with which to pay the fine. But then he was allowed to go home – without the chosen souvenirs, however.

An English schoolboy had taken twelve boxes of matches with different pictures of Paris on them. He admitted it straight away, gave them back and the whole thing was forgotten.

I lasted for just three months in the department store. By then I had had enough. Standing around for ages in high heeled shoes did not suit my feet. After that I had to wear shoes with special insoles for a while. When I took my leave of some of the other salespeople, they called after me, with a touch of envy: "Vous avez de la chance, de sauter de la boîte."

Now, when I occasionally visit Printemps, I automatically hear the bell signals whether I want to or not. Then I surprise myself by humming the Swedish Rhapsody.

But mostly I shop next door at the Galeries Lafayette where there is more choice anyway and where I somehow feel more free.

An Autumn Afternoon

As things have turned out, I now have almost no human contact any more. My daughter, though, does ring up from Paris once or twice a week. Apart from that, there is the contact with pupils, of whom I currently only have two. One, a girl, lives right next to Holland Park. I don't know that area very well, and whenever a part of this huge city of London is unfamiliar to me, I particularly enjoy going there. So, I get out at High Street Kensington and usually take a taxi to cover the short distance to the elegant row of houses in Melbury Court, adjacent to the entrance to the Commonwealth Institute and next to the exceptionally beautiful Holland Park.

I tutor her to help her prepare for her German A-level the following year. Our literary texts have been Brecht's 'Caucasian Chalk Circle', 'Andorra' by Max Frisch and Fontane's '*Delusions, Confusions*'. Today we have been reading some 'Andorra'. We got to the word 'spazierengehen' (going for a walk); the related words in German, derived from that word, such as 'a walk' and a 'walking stick', were words she did not understand. She attends the Lycée Français here, which means we can speak English, German or French, whichever is most appropriate at the time.

As today is an autumn day and we had been talking about 'going for a walk' and about France, I quite unexpectedly had a kind of memory flash, and I remembered a wonderful walk I had once taken in Paris on an unforgettably beautiful autumn day. It was in the Bois de Boulogne that this long, glorious walk happened. I marvelled at the trees and their splendidly colourful leaves. At the end of the walk, I suddenly came out of the park to find myself in the street where the Theatre des Champs Elysées was, near the Alma–Marceau Metro station. It was a warm autumn evening and a lot of people were standing outside the theatre, smoking and chatting. The doors were wide open. In the foyer there were just as many people. Suddenly one could hear a bell ringing, as if from far away.

Everybody went inside into a large auditorium. I simply went in with them, as if carried along by a cloud. I walked down the central aisle towards the front, close to the orchestra. There were a few comfortable-looking vacant seats. I just sat down. I spotted a programme on the floor: in big letters it said there 'Bamberg Symphony Orchestra'. The name of the conductor, too: Karl Böhm. The musicians were now appearing on the stage. I waited expectantly. And they played Beethoven's 8th Symphony. Beethoven had called it 'my sinfonietta'. Never before had I heard it played so beautifully, with such detail, so fresh and joyous. That afternoon, it was like a gift from life itself.

Gratefully, I applauded at the end and left the concert hall after the second part of the concert had ended, going out into the street again. Everything still felt unreal to me, almost like an out-of-body experience. And yet, where I had serendipitously ended up had been the most magnificent reality. Full of gratitude, I went home and as you, dear reader, have now found out, I have never forgotten that afternoon.

The Pupil from
Primrose Hill

An indefinable, perhaps somewhat hoarse, male voice said down the telephone: "I got your address from the H. Institute. I'd like some private German lessons. I know that the Institute charges fifty pounds an hour but I can't afford that much. I could pay twenty pounds an hour."

The person at the other end of the phone was astonished to find out how much the Institute charged but she hid her surprise and said: "Alright, that's fine, I can teach you." He gave her his address and they agreed on a particular day in the late afternoon. 'Since he named the price,' she thought, 'it should be alright.' Had it been up to her, she would never have dared to charge so much.

He lived in the area where she herself had lived on first coming to London – indeed to this country. The husband of an old friend from the former days in Berlin was called Andrew. That had been more than twenty-four years ago. By coincidence this new pupil was also called Andrew. His surname didn't suit his face. It was a neutral sounding French name. His parents lived in Manchester, where he had been born. His father was an optician and his mother also had a respectable profession. Apparently the family was well off. His grandparents belonged to the large group of Lithuanian Jews who had immigrated to the North of England, often because of pogroms in their own country. In those days they had had to find new ways of earning a living and many of them had later become wealthy members of English society. They kept up the tradition of celebrating the Jewish holidays and attending the synagogue. In time it emerged that Andrew's family surname had originally been Gstein or something similar.

He was alert, about twenty–five or twenty-six years old with frizzy hair and dark eyes behind extremely expensive Giorgio Armani spectacles with polished lenses. He lived in Chalcot Road on the fourth floor. The stairs were incredibly steep and the German teacher privately wondered how much longer she would manage to go up and down them. She took great care and climbed slowly. At the top of the stairs was a three-roomed flat, shared by three young people. It seemed to be a sort of flat-share arrangement.

The lessons went well, with no problems of any sort. He was quick to understand, was intelligent and had already learnt a bit of German at school. Unfortunately he had one slightly unpleasant habit; he tended to grab all the pens and pencils within reach and chew them up. The German teacher found this rather disgusting and each pencil she brought with her had disappeared by the end of the lesson. She added that on to her expenses. Once, she heard the manner in which he talked to his mother on the telephone and found this disturbing – or rather, she was amazed by it. Furthermore, he had the habit of praising himself at the end of each chapter. The teacher was surprised by this and thought privately: 'Don't blow your own trumpet.' However, she kept this to herself and was happy to get the twenty pounds. He paid promptly after each lesson. As one says in England, 'Pay as you go and you won't have any difficulties'.

During the day, Andrew worked as a bookkeeper with some firm and at the same time studied economics; he was preparing for exams. Every now and then he got sent to Luxembourg to do some work there. Here in London he was sometimes sent by his firm to check the book-keeping of others. Once he gave the German teacher a present. It was a calendar issued by the House of Pirastro, who had been making strings for stringed instruments since 1798. For the whole year there were pictures of one pretty girl with her huge cello; each month she smiled in a different manner and more mischievously. It was all in black and white and on each photo one could see part of her décolleté. However, she was certainly no cellist. Perhaps the creators of the calendar thought that it was good taste to use the title 'String emotions 1994'. There was also a logo consisting of two little tuning forks inside an octagon. Written in German was:

Editor:	Gustav Pirazzi and Co.
Concept and realization:	Oelenheinz and Frey, Munich
Photography:	Andreas Förg
Lithography:	Mrs. Mannheim
Print: Print II	Mannheim
Copyright:	Gustav Pirazzi and Co.

She went on like this for two and a half years. She always enjoyed walking down Fitzroy Road. On the right stood the house with the blue plaque commemorating Yeats. More recently, Sylvia Plath had also lived there. On December 14th 1962, the latter had written to her mother: 'Well, there I was, safely installed in Yeats' house: just got to the stage of being able to make a cup of tea after this enormous move…' The 12th of February was Sylvia Plath's last day alive. She did not live in that house for long. Around the corner to the left is number seven, Chalcot Square, from where Sylvia Plath wrote on the 2nd of February 1960 to her mother: 'This is the first letter to leave our new home.' She so much loved living in this part of London, near the beautiful park of Primrose Hill, Regent's Park and London Zoo, that she really wanted to move back there. At the end of 1962 she found the flat in Fitzroy Road – which was to be her last dwelling.

The False Houses

On the 21st March 1995 the teacher had to go, as usual on a Tuesday evening, to the house in Chalcot Road for the German lesson. She was a few minutes too early and stood in front of the shop window next to the house where she was expected at half-past six. She marvelled at a portrait of the very good and internationally acclaimed English film critic, Derek Malcolm. She stood there in a dream and admired the picture. Suddenly Andrew was standing next to her on the street, swinging his car key. He had to drive immediately to Heathrow Airport to pick up a friend who was to arrive soon. Although he had known about this for two days, he had not had time to tell her. All that he could do was to offer to drive her home quickly in his car. She reacted in a puzzled manner and hardly knew where to look at first. Whether to look at the portrait or at Andrew? She decided on the latter.

The Second Room

The bed stood against the wall on the right; next to it was a little table with a drawer that one could lock. Then came the large door to the balcony which could, of course, be opened so that one could go out and stand on the small balcony. It was a corner house, 150 Rue Raymond Losserand, adjoining Rue Ridder. On the opposite side of the road was the Hôpital Laennec. On a small green patch of grass was a solitary sheep or lamb. I don't know why there was only one sheep, but anyway it relieved the austerity of the view. After all, who would expect to see a little sheep suddenly, right in the middle of town? I regarded the little sheep as my neighbour, because I was also like a silly sheep, so to speak.

The Quartier was extremely popular. The room was rented from Belarussians who had fled from the Russian revolution in 1917.

"On vient et on vous prend tout,' explained Madame de Severin, the landlady, to me later on as I sat with her in her room, drinking tea sweetened with jam instead of sugar; or having Borscht, beetroot soup, which she made every now and then. Hanging on the walls were family photos, all of important military men from the Russian past, in St. Petersburg I believe. Madame de Severin was a charming lady (why did she have a French name?). Her late husband had also been Russian, a lawyer in Paris. Perhaps he had changed his name, as immigrants often do or did. Cid Corman from America – a Russian Jew – once told me how he came to be called Corman. This is how it happened: when his father arrived in North America and had to go through immigration control, the man in front of him was called Corman and so he simply chose the same name. And when my mother put my name down for the Pestalozzi school in Buenos Aires, she suddenly gave me the surname of Wolf instead of Aron. After that I always had terrible problems with my papers and it was not until I travelled back to Europe for the first time in 1950 that I called myself Aron again.

Indeed, as a young girl, Madame de Severin's surname had been Toporkoff. I know that for a fact because that is what her brothers were called. One of them lived in the same flat. He was an architect and worked in an office on the Boulevard St. Germain. The family had beautiful, well-manicured and expressive hands and they had kept up some remnants of their culture. They knew Henri Troyat, who wrote in French but originated from Russia – or at least his parents did. Madame de Severin's elder brother, Monsieur Serge, kept a small military museum in the same house, several floors up, and was able to provide Henri Troyat with a lot of material. Once a friend of mine gave me theatre tickets for a play by Chekhov (probably The Three Sisters.) One of the actors was Sacha Pitoeff who had married a Spanish friend of mine, Maricarmen. Maricarmen had, like me, lived in Buenos Aires until she won a scholarship to study acting in Paris. She was overjoyed about this and often gave us tickets for the theatre; Madame de Severin attended the performances with one of her friends and made very intelligent comments afterwards.

Once she said to me: "If you always pay the rent on time, Edith," (putting the accent on the 'i' in my name like all my French and Spanish speaking friends), "we will never have any problems". She also allowed me to hire an upright piano from Schindler and Co. I still remember how they brought it and also when they picked it up again because I was behind again with the monthly payment. But I had it for a long time; I think I lived in that room for three years. As I said before, it was a corner room with a balcony. Standing in the room was also one of those tall French cupboards with a large mirror; and there was a green armchair for me or for any unexpected visitors. I believe the right arm of this armchair was a bit wobbly or broken. But nobody noticed this. Only I knew. Next to the armchair was the door leading to the bathroom which I shared with Madame de Severin. To the left of this door stood the Schindler piano. What did I learn to play on it apart from Clementi studies? The Little Notebook of Anna Magdalena Bach, the Little Preludes and Fugues. Le Petit Nègre by Débussy. The first easy pieces by Schumann. Of course, Für Elise by Beethoven and the beginning of a Scarlatti sonata.

My Argentine friend came and played tangos on the piano. As soon as he was in the room he sat down in the armchair and – whoops – I landed on his lap.

"One can't have a serious conversation with you," he said, "you only lark around." He was frightfully intellectual, my Argentine friend, and wore spectacles made of window glass. He had been awarded a scholarship (similar to Maricarmen's acting scholarship) by the French government to study comparative literature, and lived in the Argentine pavilion at the Cité Universitaire. One afternoon he dropped by unexpectedly, bringing petit fours as a present. I got home a bit later and my diary lay open on the tiny desk. Perhaps he read something in it which rather depressed, hurt or upset him. Who knows? I don't. Perhaps it's just my imagination. Anyway, what I really wanted to do in those days was learn, learn, learn. He had found a flat for us both near the Odéon Metro station. But, as always, I didn't decide in time and let the deadline expire. Nevertheless, it was the most beautiful time that I ever had. I had a little plant in my room; I believe he also had the same sort of plant. We called it 'plantita'. That is Spanish for 'little plant'.

Once he said: "Come to think of it, the only living things in this room are the plant, you and me."

Another time I said: "If we have a house or flat one day, will we have a dog as well?" He burst into loud peals of laughter, but I was just surprised by his reaction.

He made a list of all the books that it was important for me to read, because I wanted to educate myself. I would ask: "What do the words 'professional' and 'surreal' mean?" and he could always explain them to me wonderfully. Once I said to him: "Paraces un professor" ('You are like a professor.')

He answered: "Soy un professor." ('I _am_ a professor'). And sometimes he added: "I have helped many young people on their way."

And also he often said: "The year fifty-two wasn't such a bad year." I never quite understood what he meant by that.

Later he worked for a while for someone on the corner of Rue Raymond Losserand and the Rue d'Alésia. It was an office which imported and exported books. During that time he always came to lunch and I cooked. Sometimes, when we didn't have so much to talk about, he would play around with the bread-crumbs and look at me thoughtfully. I had a terrible complex about him because he knew so much whereas I knew so little and only wanted to learn. It ended up with a Pygmalion-type situation – which, however, had a different ending. And that's all I want to say about my mysterious, magical friend. But it is to him that I dedicate this chapter.

New Bond Street

"One moment please, I'll just have a quick look at my diary. Come in the first week of January, on the 4th January 1993. No," he immediately corrected himself, "let's forget the first week, it would be better for us to begin on Monday the 11th January in the lunch break at half past twelve in my office in New Bond Street. I'll just tell you the address again a bit more clearly: it's 150 New Bond Street, on the corner of Conduit Street. It's Ireland House. You'll recognise the green, white and orange flag even from a distance. It's always hanging outside. My office is on the second floor. Downstairs at the entrance you'll have to sign your name in a book and you'll get a little plastic card with a number on it. Take the lift up to the second floor. The lady at reception will inform me straightaway."

She did all that the voice on the telephone had told her to do and was looking forward to the job in this area of London which was still quite unfamiliar to her – by far the most elegant part of this world-famous city. The most beautiful and most expensive shops are almost all concentrated in New Bond Street. Now, what are they all called? On the corner of Brook Street and New Bond Street is the Emporio Armani with the most chic and costly clothes one could possibly imagine. Opposite is Fenwicks with the most splendid international models, and where one can find bargains twice a year in the sales. On the other side of the street, at number

103, is Nelson House, formerly frequented by Lady Chatterley. On the ground floor is a shop called Red-Green of Scandinavia. And next to it are the Bally Galleries with Late Fine Art and an antiques centre. On the other side of the street again is the White House shop selling high-class bed linen, pyjamas, elegant nightwear and bathrobes for adults and children. Next to it, at number 59, is the music shop, Chappell of Bond Street, which has existed since 1811. Earlier we often used to go there to buy music and clarinet reeds for my daughter. Then there is a shop called Canale-Milano with exclusive gentlemen's clothing and upstairs in the same house one can buy antique maps and atlases at Jonathan Potter. In the shop window of Bruno Magli are especially beautiful shoes and leather jackets and on the corner opposite, a branch of the Midland Bank, more incredibly elegant shoes at Pinet. We go on a bit further and there is Sotheby's, where auctions of great works of art are often held. The most interesting books on art and often very good pictures are always exhibited in the window. And diagonally opposite is the shop which always fascinated me anew. It is SJ Phillips Ltd., 139 Bond Street, selling, as described on the shop front, 'Antique Silver, Fine Jewels, Miniatures, Snuff Boxes, By Appointment Antique Dealer to Queen Elizabeth, the Queen Mother and the late Queen Mary', with the appropriate coat of arms for the English throne – the lion on the left and the unicorn on the right. Whenever I passed this shop I always stopped and looked at the antique diamond rings. One day I discovered an oval- shaped diamond ring covered all over with cut squares and set in green emeralds. It seemed to me that I knew this ring. My childhood friend, Irma Strauss, had inherited this ring from her mother and had always worn it after her death. That was in 1937. It was a most beautiful ring. After my own mother died, I had her diamond ring, which was similar even though it was round and not oval, also set in emeralds.

Each time I passed this shop I looked out for the ring of my old childhood friend. It was something that I really knew, something which came from a different country, something that connected me with my past and my youth. I passed by, saw the ring and was happy. Upstairs in Ireland House I was always welcomed respectfully. In the reception area stood a large, tastefully selected bouquet of flowers. The receptionist would tell Herr Connelly, in her Irish accent, that I was there and he always came down quickly. We would go into the room which was ready for us, sitting down at the big table which was otherwise used for conferences. I sat at the end and he sat on my right. On the walls were landscapes of Ireland with little owls sitting in the trees. From where I sat, one could see Conduit Street on the left and the elegant Conduit Hotel. Aribert Reimann stayed there when he came to London for the performance of one of his works – it might even have been his opera, 'King Lear', which was performed by English National Opera near Trafalgar Square – or perhaps it was his 'Ghost Sonata' which was played in one of the large concert halls on the South Bank. It was a pleasant hotel, not one of those exaggeratedly luxurious hotels for tourists.

Herr Connelly had already been learning German, without a textbook, from a young architecture student, who, however, had gone back to Germany. He wanted to learn German because he was hoping to be transferred to Ireland House in Düsseldorf. That was his aim. He was at that time thirty-nine or forty years old, looked older, had lost some of his already white hair. On the left side of his mouth he was missing an incisor which it didn't occur to him to replace and he had either a small beard or maybe only a moustache. I never looked at him with the thought that I might one day be describing him. His arms and hands were young, strong and pleasing, as was his whole figure. He was perhaps 1.78 metres tall, a good size, with a rather sporty, agreeable look.

He always greeted me with the words: "Good morning" followed by "What would you like to drink? Tea, coffee, water?" And then he brought the chosen drinks in small cardboard cups. His ties were sometimes in very good taste but sometimes most doubtful. I never really found out what his work was and I never asked him directly, although we sometimes translated business letters. He had something to do with the Irish Chamber of Commerce and frequently had to travel around the country to big trade fairs. He often went to Manchester and Birmingham as well as Scotland and Dublin, from Stansted airport. The flight took half an hour. He had been married for five years; his wife – also Irish – was a music teacher in a school for young children out in Milton Keynes where they lived. So every day he travelled an hour by train to London. He said it didn't matter, there were always enough seats and he could use the time for studying. The lessons were lively, never boring; he had a good sense of humour and he learnt well, easily and with interest. From time to time he mentioned the job in Düsseldorf which was due to come up. Then he would take additional lessons in the evenings after office hours. His thirty-five-year-old wife was expecting her first baby soon. He often stayed at home to help her, although they were well off and could have afforded a home help. Furthermore, a sister of his wife lived next door. Generally he seemed a bit worried about his wife. I was surprised that he missed work so often just because his wife seemed to demand it of him. Later on, he was occasionally somewhat tired in the mornings. He explained that it was because the child often woke in the night and was hungry and he had to give it its bottle.

The lessons were mostly in the lunch hour, sometimes two or three times a week depending on the possibility of the job in Germany.

On my way there, I always kept an eye out for the ring which lay in the shop window of SJ Phillips Ltd. Sometimes it wasn't there. That would give me a fright. It would disappear suddenly for months on end and then one day, there it would be lying again, on a little velvet cushion. When it was there I felt reassured. That reminded me of the film 'Breakfast at Tiffany's'. The display at Tiffany's gave the main character in the film a feeling of security. The sight of the ring had a similar effect on me. A continuation of something, a link to the past, to the first years of my youth in Buenos Aires. England was now the fourth country in which I had lived. I walked along Bond Street to my German lesson. I got a friendly reception at Ireland House. Even the name which I had to enter in the visitors' book downstairs was Irish. In James Joyce's book 'The Dubliners', there was also a Mrs. Bergin. That was the surname of my English identity.

That was the name which was in her English passport. The name, in which everything was set up and with which everything functioned in this fourth country. Still, she wasn't allowed to do, and could not do, without her maiden name. She had become something like two persons in one, and she had got used to this over the years.

Once the ring vanished for several months. One day she plucked up courage and went into the exclusive shop. At the door stood a guard in uniform. A salesman with a highly distinguished manner – Mr. Judd – approached her immediately. She described the ring as well as she could and the grand salesman went to a glass cabinet towards the back of the shop and brought the ring straightaway on a purple velvet cushion. She breathed a sigh of relief. There was the ring, safe as ever.

"What does this ring cost?"

"Six thousand pounds. It is an especially precious ring from the year 1937."

"It wasn't in the shop window for a long time."

"Yes, sometimes we change rings over or put them in a different place – down there on the right, for instance."

The ring was there, all was well. Life could go on. Of course she was not in the least interested in owning the ring; nevertheless she said, for form's sake, that she had to consult someone about the price.

"It is a rare and valuable ring." said the salesman and gave her his hand-signed visiting card. For two and a half years she walked along New Bond Street, always casting a glance towards the window in which the ring lay. Sometimes it had disappeared for a while and then all of a sudden it would be lying in its place again on the pretty velvet cushion. If it was there, she was happy. If not, she waited for it to come back.

From time to time Herr Connelly spoke about the job in Düsseldorf which was due to come up in the autumn. He took more lessons, as he would be required to sit an exam in Dublin. Then he announced that the job in Düsseldorf was not the right one for him after all; he would have to wait until the spring, when a more senior position would become available.

They worked through the six German course books together. Newspaper articles and everything needed for advanced lessons. When the chance of a job seemed more distant there were fewer lessons. By now she had got to know all the office rooms and all the floors of Ireland House because every now and then the building was renovated. As ever, she liked going to this elegant part of London. Sometimes it seemed to her as though the ring knew her and twinkled at her. Who knows, perhaps it was the same ring – perhaps the Belgian husband of her friend had sold it after the premature death of his wife and it had ended up in this antique jeweller's shop in London. After all, had it not been confirmed to her that the ring was made in 1937?

After the lesson at midday she always went to eat at the little Italian snack bar, Licensed Restaurant No. 56 Maddox Street, opposite the elegant gentlemen's outfitters Rossini. It was one of those typical Italian restaurants which are squeezed into the tiniest space. It consisted of four large-ish tables, each with four chairs and one more round table, also provided, when necessary, with four chairs. In spite of the lack of space, everything worked wonderfully. The food was cheap, got served quickly, and was good. The owner – Italian of course – stood behind the counter, was always friendly, and was honestly pleased if one returned regularly. The waitress was a Signora Aurora, small, deft and always in good spirits. She was the life and soul of the place. She reminded her of Madame Simoné from Paris in the fifties, and of the Restaurant Odéon in the Passage Rohan, which had since become an expensive restaurant. In those days, Madame Simoné was the main reason for going to that restaurant. She greeted everyone as warmly as if they were her family. On her day off she sometimes invited her favourite customers to her own home for a meal. Whenever one of the customers who was an artist had his first Paris exhibition, she would display his poster on the wall. The same went for young up-and-coming writers with their first publications. We sat there with Cortázar, with Sergio de Castro and Marta Mosquera, and with many other friends and artists who lived there between 1950 and 1954.

Of course, it was different here. She didn't know anyone. Only the tall young man who worked next door in the reception area at Sotheby's. He always came in at about three in the afternoon.

She often ordered the same dish. Spaghetti bolognese followed by fruit salad. It was cheap and tasted good. And it was so nice, she was greeted as 'Senora' and people spoke a few words of Spanish to her. No-one knew that she was now a German teacher. Because the owners were, like her, foreigners in England, they sometimes watched the same television programmes on Sundays. For example, they talked about Peter Ustinov's last series about old churches and castles, filmed in Italy.

On the walls were some photos of people she didn't know. Also reproductions of little landscapes, sunflowers, or groups of cottages in front of a lake with reeds. In the alcoves stood old wine bottles covered with raffia.

Opposite Rossini was a shop called Cashmere Shop. The things on display were not particularly beautiful but were expensive all the same. Next door was Smythson of Bond Street, established in 1887, where one could get the most elegant notepaper in the world. Once I bought an extremely luxurious pocket diary made of the finest leather, reduced from twenty pounds to eight. It was cheaper because it was already the third month of the year, March. I said: "I won't pay more than five pounds" and to my great astonishment they immediately agreed. A prince from Saudi Arabia always bought his posh Christmas cards there. This shop proudly displays three coats of arms. Underneath them it says three times over: 'By appointment to Her Majesty the Queen, Queen Elizabeth and the Queen Mother and his Royal Highness, the Prince of Wales, Suppliers of Stationery and Office Equipment, Frank Smythson, London.'

On the other side of the road is Yves Saint Laurent, rive gauche, framed by Renoir House, No. 135-137. Then comes, as already mentioned, SJ Phillips Ltd. Next to it is the gentlemen's outfitters Zilli with coats and furs. Opposite is Richard Green Old Art and opposite yet again is Maltett with antique classic furniture with, on the first floor of the same house, Christopher Wood, Paintings. Next door, the very expensive fashion shop, Ralph Lauren. At Herberto Johnson there are the most unusual hats for ladies and gentlemen as well as extravagant umbrellas, dressing gowns and sports jackets. Then again, period furniture opposite at Patride. Number 147 is the world-famous Galerie Wilderstein, Fine Works of Art. Then the silversmith Tessiers. Next to that is Louis Vuitton with fine leatherwares, followed by Hermes Paris, Ballantine and Max Mara Fashions.

Now we are in the upper part of Old Bond Street, standing in front of a stone bench right in the middle of the street. On top of it sit two life-sized statues: Churchill with his cigar in his hand and Roosevelt, apparently having a lively discussion together. We decipher the signature of the sculptor: L. Holot Cenfor. Placement and dedication date: the 50th jubilee of VE Day or Victory in Europe Day, 1995.

The job for which Herr Connelly had been waiting in the spring was given to someone else. However, at around the same time his wife presented him with a second baby.

Is the ring still lying in the shop window at SJ Phillips?

We don't know because we hardly ever go to New Bond Street nowadays.

The Visitor and the Very Old Lady

Today would have been her mother's birthday. Although her mother had died a long time ago, of course she never forgot the date. So she took her grandmother's vase out of the cupboard; this vase had crossed the ocean twice, all safely wrapped up. Once when they had emigrated and again when they came back. Her mother had given this vase to her own mother as a present at the age of twelve. She bought some expensive sweet peas, which she knew her mother had particularly liked. She put them all in the small vase and, using the scissors which she had inherited from her mother, cut a bit off the base of the stems. Then she placed the vase on the window sill, put the scissors next to it and also put the cut-off green stems in a glass of water. She could not quite work out why this made her think of the amputated leg of the ninety-one year-old husband of an acquaintance in Germany.

Right, and now I'll go out, she said to herself resolutely. I'll go and visit the ninety-six year-old poetess who lives in this same city. A thirty-minute bus ride and I'll be there. No sooner said than done. She took with her a packet of the good biscuits that she used to buy in a Viennese bakery. The first time she had been to the bakery, she had bought the same kind of 'Plätzchen'. They had a very special taste. She also took a continental sausage and German liver paté because the old lady still loved German sausages, even after fifty-five years in exile, and she still wrote poetry in her native German language. Being in exile had hardly affected her. She lived alone in her house in a quiet street in the north of the city. "Don't tell anyone that I live here alone despite being so very old." she said once.

Every Sunday her seventy-three-year-old son picked her up in his car and drove her to his family home for a meal. She was, of course, a grandmother and even a great-grandmother. Her first husband, the father of the son, had died fifty years previously. She had remarried and, several years earlier, had been widowed again. Once the son, who had become a businessman, said: "At least I have no problems with inheritance." He had a great sense of humour and this was a light-hearted reference to his poet parents. His mother got older and older and of course he did too. He visited her as often as he could, always brought her flowers, and read her post out loud to her because her eyes were no longer so good, due to her extreme old age. And so the old lady lived alone with a cat in the two-storey house, with its back garden and little front garden. Apart from the gardener, who came regularly and pruned whatever there was to prune, a cleaning lady came once or twice a week. It was a pretty house. The furniture dated from the twenties and came from Berlin. There one could find old editions of books from that time, and letters from famous contemporaries; and there was a picture of Ludwig Meidner on the wall.

For hours on end the old lady would crush the cat food with a fork on a plastic or tin plate in the kitchen, mashing it for ages until it got really mushy. The cat could hardly wait to get its food at long last. And then it was gone in a trice. Once the lady told me how she came to get this cat. The cat had secretly strayed into her house and, at first, hid for days under the carpet. One day a visitor noticed that some living creature was moving under the carpet. They both had a look and, lo and behold, there was a beautiful white Siamese cat.

Well, as usual on a Saturday afternoon, our visitor went to

see the ninety-six-year-old poetess, this time armed with the book: 'Letters from Great Poets to their Mothers.' She had given her own mother this same book twenty-five years ago when her mother had had to stay in hospital for six months. The latter had been thrilled with this present; it really was a wonderful collection of letters. Sometimes she wrote little poems of her own, though not for publication. Nonetheless, she had noted down some telephone numbers on the last blank pages of the book, which were immediately noticed by the old lady.

"Shall I read you a letter?"

"Yes, but only a short one."

Then the old lady related all the good news which she had received from Germany, sighing at the same time, that it would have been better for her if all that was happening to her now had happened twenty years ago.

"So today would have been your mother's birthday?"

"Yes, today she would have been the same age as you, ninety-six!" And without really realising what she was doing, she got up and gave the old lady a light kiss on her white hair.

Then the old lady asked her to read out a few of her more recent poems. Our visitor said that she would type them out for her and enlarge the photocopies so that the old lady could read them herself; she would send them to her on the Monday or Tuesday.

Now the old lady suddenly reacted in an unexpected manner and, although obviously meaning well in a motherly sort of way, started asking her personal questions which probed too deeply and made her feel uncomfortable.

So she said goodbye rather hastily. On the way to the bus stop she saw a solitary, extremely elegant, dark reddish-brown leather shoe, Charles Jourdan, Paris label, high-heeled and completely new. She saw it lying there on the ground and continued on her way. When she was waiting on the Finchley Road for the bus, there lay the other shoe on the pavement, all on its own. She went back to where the first shoe lay, picked it up, went back to the

Finchley Road, picked up the other one, put them in a plastic bag and took the elegant, unworn pumps, made out of finest leather, home with her.

On the journey home she thought to herself that perhaps it hadn't been the right place to commemorate her mother's birthday after all.

Fireworks

It all began on the Pont Neuf during the fireworks display on July 14th, when the 'Great Star' was let off into the night sky. The crowd around us, consisting of perhaps 70% French and 30% foreigners, greeted each flash in the sky with enthusiastic aaaahs and oooohs. "Que c'est beau!" All at once I heard someone next to me say in German: "Watch out that your hair doesn't burn – a spark could fall on to it!" I turned around and found myself looking into a face with a moustache, large dark eyes, black hair and rather dark skin. I was surprised that someone with such southern looks should speak German without an accent and, at the same time, thought to myself that it was rather a shame that I wasn't on my own. Still, had I been unaccompanied, the man would not have heard us speaking German and would not have spoken to me; also, thanks to my companion, it was fine for me to answer him.

"Are you German?" I asked, somewhat surprised.

"Yes." he replied.

'He doesn't look like a student,' I thought.

"Ooooh, c'est la grande" cried the crowd and then "Aaaaaah, it's the basket of flowers!" Then came ten bangs, one after the other, and in the sky appeared blue, white and red sparks – the Tricolor – to show that the display had now come to the end.

The crowd dispersed in various directions and the man came

with us, as if it were the most natural thing in the world. First we crossed over to the Quai Malaquais, sat down on the stone wall by the river bank and admired the play of the shadows thrown on the house walls by the Bateau Mouche, which was making its eleven o'clock circuit. Then we introduced ourselves to each other.

"Ah, you're Herr So-and-So? It's such a small world. I've heard a lot about you and also, that you've just moved from Berlin to Paris. Herr C., who, as we know, also lives here, was talking to me about you just a few days ago."

We had already found something in common and all felt relieved.

"My wife is in Switzerland with her family at the moment. I've been working at home the whole day and felt like going out; I wanted to be nearer to the fireworks."

Then the three of us walked along the Seine to the Place Hôtel de Ville. But there were so many people there that my companion suggested driving around the city for a bit in his car until we found a place where we felt like stopping. At last we pushed our way through to the Place de Vosges. Four musicians were playing eagerly on a little stage set up in the corner of the square. And everything was decorated with coloured light bulbs and little flags. In front of the stage, there was a dance floor, with couples dancing enthusiastically. We watched for a while without joining in. Every now and then my companion said that he was terribly tired; after all, he had been sitting behind the steering wheel of his car for eight hours since leaving Stuttgart at seven that morning, and he was flying off to Algiers the next afternoon, in a specially chartered plane. We hardly knew each other; he had got my address from the Saarland Radio, was spending the night in a hotel on the Rue St Louis en Île and had dropped by that evening on the off-chance of meeting me and saying hello. Then we had decided to walk to the Pont Neuf to see the fireworks.

Herr So-and-So asked me to dance. We hardly spoke to each other. I could feel his hand. "Spin faster" was all he said to me. When the dance ended and we returned to our places, my companion said: "Please excuse me, but I'm just too tired to stay any longer. I'll come to you at breakfast tomorrow morning and bring a baguette, if that's alright by you?"

"Yes." I said. "Come at nine. I hope you don't mind if I stay here a bit longer? It's so nice!"

And then we danced, Herr So-and-So and I, one dance after the other. Every now and then we sat down and had a cool drink.

"I've rather fallen in love," he said suddenly. I didn't say anything but I felt happy. At last, just the sort of Bastille Day I had always wished for.

"Let's go for a short walk," he suggested. We walked hand in hand through the dark streets of the Marais down to the banks of the Seine. There we went down the steps to the river. Without much searching for a space, we sat down under a tree. It was a weeping willow.

"I live just over there," I said and pointed to a little window on the top floor of a house.

After a while we climbed the steps again and crossed over the Pont Marie to the house. When we got up to the top floor he said: "You live in a beautiful place." Then he looked for something on the bookshelf and handed it to me.

The next morning, as arranged, someone knocked on the door, baguette in hand and was fairly surprised not to find me on my own.

After breakfast, we went down to the street and parted until the evening. I went with the Stuttgart man to the Foreign Ministry, as I had promised on the previous day, to translate something for him. After that we went to the Invalides Airport to find a parking space for his car which he was to pick up on his return from Africa. In the very best of moods, I wished him a good flight!

When I got home I suddenly tossed everything out of the drawers, emptied out the cupboard, put on one gramophone record after the other, found, whilst tidying up, the self-portrait of Cézanne and put it on the top shelf of the bookshelf because I suddenly thought it looked rather like Herr ****. All at once, I wanted to polish everything, clean out even the smallest corners and put everything in order. I felt as though I was newly born.

Towards half past seven, there was a knock at the door. He was rather astonished by all the mess and the changes in the room.

After supper he told me that he had an especially nice wife and that she was staying with her parents and expecting a baby. He was going to join her in two weeks' time.

Two weeks – fourteen days. That was how it was and that was how it stayed.

The Dark Blue Suit or Independence

Lucia Menhard, or Pauline, was a girl who got sent out to work as soon as she had taken her final exam at primary school. Her mother, who had brought her up in this new country in South America – the father had stayed in Europe – could not afford to send her to secondary school and perhaps did not realise how important that would be for her daughter's future. Using the money that her parents had given her earlier in Germany – a sort of second dowry to help her build a life in the new country – her mother opened a small hotel, or rather, a sort of guest house, where the guests could eat at midday and in the evenings. It was a spacious apartment on two floors with an elegant roof garden, situated fairly centrally in a more or less good area of Buenos Aires, near the Plaza San Martin. The apartment had at one time apparently belonged to none less than President Uriburu. It was so splendid. There were ten rooms, two or three bathrooms, a large entrance hall and a top floor with a roof garden. The address of the house was Charcas 883, on the corner of Suipacha Street. Nothing was left from the former president's occupation apart from a plaque on the house, but opposite, on Suipacha Street there was now a large mansion set in a big park containing beautiful, impressive trees with powerful roots and the most exotic songbirds.

In front of it a few soldiers were always keeping guard. Nowadays it was again occupied by a president. His name was Ortiz. I am talking here about the middle of the thirties and the beginning of the forties in Buenos Aires. Up on the roof garden, the girl kept a sort of mini-zoo of pets; she spent a lot of time up there and had a good view over the president's park opposite. She had bought a lovely birdcage for her four budgerigars. People advised her to clip their wings so that if their door was left open they could not fly away. She did not believe them and all four flew off into the park. That gave her an excuse to go into the president's park, but the birds never returned. She had a separate cage for her canary which had the German name of Hansi.

Her Uncle Carlos, who had emigrated to Argentina in the twenties and his wife, Caroline, from Breslau, also had a large aviary. Whenever Pauline visited them in the long summer holidays she took her canary with her on the fifteen-hour train journey to Villa Iris, right on the border of the Pampas province. At the house next door was a parrot, always sitting in the garden and which, whenever a female of any description passed by, called out: "Adios Rubia!" (Hello, my beauty!). Hansi soon found a girlfriend in Uncle Carlos's large aviary, called Palomita. When we left to go home at the end of the holidays, Hansi hardly uttered a single chirp in his cage. He would much rather have stayed there. And fairly soon after, when I came home from school one day, I found him lying lifeless in his cage.

Uncle Carlos was the local dentist and his wife was a dental technician. It was at their house that Pauline read the book 'Don Segundo Sombra', the story of a Gaucho by Ricardo Guiraldes (1882-1927) and also fragments of another Gaucho ballad, 'Martin Fierro' by José Hernandez (1834-1886). She was amused by Uncle Carlos' belt which he never wanted to take off. On it engraved in big silver letters was his name, CARLOS. He and his wife had always wanted to return to Germany and had saved up for many years; however, they had to change their plans because of the war, and in the end the rest of their family joined them by emigrating to Argentina. So Uncle Carlos was the pioneer. Pauline always enjoyed her summer holidays there. Her uncle wanted her to follow him in his profession and would have paid for her studies but of course that came to nothing. His practice was in the village but he also had two little cases full of dental tools and a portable, collapsible drill. These he transported in his thirties' car, similar to a jeep, so that he could visit the people living on isolated farms in the Pampas. Each house, including Uncle Carlos's house in the village, had its own windmill – otherwise they would not have had any running water. The people who had lived there for years, or had been born there, all had rather damaged, light brown teeth because of the water. Sometimes Pauline drove with him to visit the Munk family, who had also originally come from Germany. Frau Munk still baked German cakes and her filter coffee tasted good. Also, they had a gramophone from the thirties and used to play their favourite song on it: 'Die Fenster auf, der Lenz ist da' ('Open the windows, Spring has come')

The Munk family still spoke with the accent of their homeland. The only clock in the house was a sizeable alarm clock. On one occasion Frau Munk had to go to hospital, maybe in Bahia or even as far away as Buenos Aires, and took the alarm clock with her.

"How will you know what time it is?" said Uncle Carlos to Herr Munk, or, as he called him, Cousin Munk.

"I'll tell by the sun," he replied. One day Cousin Munk had an appointment with Uncle Carlos in the village at eleven o'clock in the morning but he didn't appear until four in the afternoon. Everyone was surprised – somewhat amazed and amused at the same time.

Back again in Buenos Aires, Pauline was obliged, like her other cousins, to earn money after finishing primary school. The simplest way was to become a nanny. One did not need special skills and the work was not particularly difficult or degrading. So she escorted the children of rich parents to the park. Her first job was in the elegant Santa-Fé Street where her aunt had opened a fashion boutique. Her aunt's business partner was called Fred, and they called the shop after him. At first it was just the two of them making the clothes, but as time went on they built up a good reputation and the business flourished. Soon there was a workshop with several seamstresses sitting around the large cutting table. There was, of course, a dressing room with big mirrors on the walls and a reception room with beautiful, comfortable armchairs for the increasing numbers of upper class customers. And the latest model was always displayed in a glass cabinet.

For weeks now, a dark blue suit had been hanging in this cabinet. It had a simple bell-shaped skirt. The jacket had tightly-fitting sleeves according to the fashion of that time and the round collar was made of several layers, decoratively stitched together with lighter-coloured thread. The jacket buttoned down the middle and the many buttons were covered in matching dark blue material. If one wanted, the jacket could be worn without a blouse underneath it. As an accessory there was a smart red and green silk scarf, extremely elegant and imported directly from Paris. Or one could wear a very fine, gossamer-thin blouse underneath it. Whenever Pauline went to see her aunt in the nearby boutique she would marvel at this suit. Once she even dared to ask if she might be allowed to try it on and she was given permission. It fitted her like a glove. She longed to own something like that. One day when she came in after an absence of some weeks, there was the dark blue suit, which had been tailor-made for a customer, still hanging in its glass cabinet. She looked at her aunt and then at the suit again. "Why is it still hanging there?" she asked.

"Well, just fancy, the client still hasn't picked up this suit though it's so pretty and made-to-measure. And, what's worse, she's moved without leaving a forwarding address. And now we're landed with it. I'll never take on work again without getting a deposit first."

Pauline pressed her handbag closer to her. She had just received her first month's pay. And a thought flashed through her head.

"Tell me, Auntie Lottie, how much would you sell this suit for?" Her aunt looked at her, speechless for a second, open-mouthed. Then she said: "Yes, of course, now you're earning a good salary. You can have it for one hundred pesos."

Pauline pulled the bank notes out of her handbag. "Here you are" she said and gave her the money. Her aunt opened the glass door of the cabinet with her little key and handed her the suit, together with the smart scarf. She put it on immediately and felt wonderful. Now she really was someone, no one could take that away from her. She would never forget this as long as she lived. Her first piece of elegant clothing, bought with money that she had earned herself.

Now several years had passed and the dark blue suit with the prettily stitched round collar had become a mere symbol in her mind. She had not been forced to take out strangers' babies in their prams for a long time; instead she had her own.

Briskly, she pushed the pram along. The baby lay in it, prettily dressed in pink. 'Tiddlywinks' had been the father's nickname for her since she was tiny. She had already learnt to laugh and sit up and soon she would be trying to walk. She was now fifteen months old and they lived in England, on Blenheim Road in a suburb of Birmingham. The first park in which they used to go for walks in those days was called Green Park.

But by now they had been in this country for a long time; everything had gone wrong and they were often obliged to accept help from strangers. They had remained poor. The mother was turning into a stooped and sad looking figure.

The dark blue suit of those former times was worn by all sorts of people, but not by her.

Six Letters

One week before Easter, he had to go abroad. "You have to decide before I leave" he kept saying. She did not have to make a decision because she had already done so long before, but he still had not given up hope. Then he left, writing her a letter before leaving town because there was no one else to whom he could say goodbye. He wrote her a second letter from Munich, where he was having a break from his journey, because there was no one else to whom he could write. A third from Linz, his lecture had gone very well, a fourth from Vienna, his former flat and old friends were no longer any use to him, his life had moved on so much in recent times, he would return soon, in fact he would be back in time for Easter. And a short postscript: 'I have transferred some money just in case'.

In the meantime she had written to him once. 'Oh well' she said to herself. 'I cooked for him every day for three months, I gave him everything I had and then he went and married someone else.'

Instead of a fifth letter, three postcards arrived. 'Dear N., I lived here in this house; the café I often visited is on this street, and on the third postcard you can see the restaurant where I usually ate. I'll be back on Friday. Please ring me.'

But she put it off until Saturday.

In the morning, at breakfast, she listened to the news as usual.

'On the motorway to Berlin there were several car accidents due to the Easter holiday traffic.' As if from far away, she heard the announcer say that one of the cars had had the registration number Berlin C805.

'Is it my fault?' she asked herself and stared aghast at the small transistor radio. Just then the doorbell rang; it was the postman. He brought the sixth letter – this time there was a stamp with a Berlin postmark on the blue envelope.

She put the letter away, switched on the radio again and went on comfortably with her breakfast.

The Golden Lion

(For John Bergin)

I was already twenty-five years old and still living in the small, narrow house at 7, Maple Street, Middlesbrough, Yorkshire. My sister and I had been born in this same house. Immediately on the right when one came in was a room which later had a piano in it. Then there was the kitchen with its cupboard, more like a room which was part of the kitchen. Behind it, outside, was the lavatory (not to use the nasty word 'bog'), in a little wooden shelter, a problem in the winter when it got very cold. And it really did get cold there. Then there was a tiny back yard where one could put up a washing line. All the houses in our street looked the same. Someone once remarked that Lowry's paintings were full of houses like that. That could be true. People tended to put objects on their window sills but we only put potted plants on ours. Upstairs on the first floor were the bedrooms. One for my parents and one for my sister and me whilst we were still children. I was one year older than her. Later on, when she was older, she got the better room and I got the room with the piano. My father had been born in Ireland and had come over to the north of England to look for work. He found some at the IBM factory, soon got to know my mother, and they got married. It was a marriage of love and we children apparently turned out well.

However, my father's work at the factory completely exhausted him. When he came home he just slept and we had to keep quiet. Once a week he would put the housekeeping money on the table. My mother always laughed a lot with us and was good-humoured. Once she was given a sewing machine for Christmas and after that she made lovely clothes for us. Another year, my sister was given a gramophone and I got a bicycle. My father bought himself a record. It was Ravel's 'Bolero' and he listened to it over and over again.

There were always lots of children living on our street and we all played together. One day during the war my little playmate got hit by a bomb; that was hard and I mourned him for a long time.

Later, when I was older and had to do military service after the Second World War, I got sent to Düsseldorf. My father accompanied me to the station and sent me on my way with some words of advice. That is my best memory of him. Otherwise he was actually not particularly nice to me and often hit me on the head. When he realised that I was interested in painting and wanted to go to art school he said: "If you want to paint, go and decorate houses like your Uncle George, who emigrated to America. He earns good money."

So I became an apprentice and learnt to be a decorator. Being young, the tedious work made me aggressive. My sister can tell stories about how my character changed at that time, how I behaved when I got back from work. But then I went to evening school and signed up for an art course.

My friend, Clive Barker, who was interested in the theatre, was allowed to go to a special school, which he enjoyed. Even my sister got financial help to study and became a teacher. I was the only one who had to do mind-numbing work.

Every time my sister and Clive came back to Middlesbrough for Easter or Christmas, I longed to go back with them to try my luck in London. My mother understood me and said: "You can go; I'm not on my own here – after all, my brother and my niece May live here and I've got lots of good friends, you know that.

And anyway, I always go to the pub on the corner in the evenings whether you're here or not."

So I wrote to Clive, who had found work in Joan Littlewood's theatre group. He replied with enthusiasm. "Just come and I'll help you get work; you can live at my place at first and we'll share the costs." In the meantime he had got to know many interesting people and talked about 'Centre 42' which had been founded by Sheila Delaney and Brendan Behan from Ireland.

In the spring of 1953 I travelled to London with high expectations and great hopes. Clive had a room in the East End on New Road. I had heard a lot about it but had never seen it. I was surprised that he had not found anywhere better to live. He was hardly ever at home and helped me much less than promised. Every now and then he got me a job at the theatre. Once I put chairs on the stage for Ionesco's play 'The Chairs', and in Beckett's 'Godot' I helped Lucky to get dressed.

Soon I felt lonely, for I wasn't suited to the life of a big city. I hardly saw anything of my sister and her friends. They lived on the other side of London. So sometimes I went for walks in the evenings. But what I saw on the streets was anything but encouraging.

On the corner of Burslem Street and Commercial Road I discovered a pub that I quite liked. It was called 'The Golden Lion' – near Cable St. and Hessel St., not far from Whitechapel Underground station.

Evening after evening, I went to the pub. I felt at home there and no longer so lonely. On the walls were pictures by the Impressionists, of course reproductions, including a painting by Gauguin. But what attracted me most of all was Eileen, behind the bar. A beautiful young girl, always friendly, the daughter of the landlord. Actually I only went to that pub because of her. Soon we got into conversation and I got to like her more and more. We often drank a gin and tonic together and she seemed to like talking to me. I wondered how to get to know her better and, one evening, asked her if I might paint her portrait. She was somewhat surprised but thought it a good idea and suggested that we begin the next week. On that evening she seemed rather nervous and drained her glasses of gin and tonic quickly, one after another.

When a few days later, I entered the pub full of optimism and new courage and asked for Eileen, the people looked at me strangely. "Oh God." they said. "Don't you know what happened since you were last here?"

"No, I haven't a clue. I want to start painting her portrait today, that's what we arranged."

"Eileen isn't alive any more. She took her own life. An unhappy love affair that she apparently couldn't get over."

Like a beaten hound, I left the pub where I had felt more or less alright.

On the very next day I moved to a different part of London and started a job in my 'trained occupation'.

A Visitor From the Past

She emerged from the room which had been assigned to her as a bedroom and, smiling and yawning at the same time, said: "Good morning!" in a very friendly way. But what was she doing here? She rubbed her right foot on the floor. Only it wasn't even a proper floor, just a shabby old carpet with rolled up corners. Everything was hard and uncomfortable. She had already been awake for hours but had not wanted to wake up the other two. At night she had to put the two worn-out mattresses on the floor. The bedsprings were completely broken and she needed a firm surface to lie on because of her bad back. On the whole, this friend from the past did not seem to have changed. But she had put off visiting her year after year and when she had been in America this Spring and had wanted to visit her at long last, the friend had cancelled, promising to make it work another time. After all, she was always busy.

And now she had missed a good opportunity to cancel the visit on her side. But she did not feel like it. She was looking forward enormously to seeing this friend after more than eleven years – but then, she always had been rather dependent on this mighty friend from her teenage years, who came from a very good family. She had learnt some manners there and, when they were teenagers, it had made a change from her home where she shared a room with her mother. The friend had always been the dominant

65

one, of course, and many people could not quite understand why these two girls, from such very different social backgrounds, should be such close friends.

So, how could they start to build on what remained of their lives? They kept talking about the past. As far as the present was concerned, they did not have so much in common, apart from the fact that they had both become language teachers and each spoke to their child in a third language.

But the hostess now completely forgot that she had a visitor in her house. Her inner life was in such a chaotic state that she did not know if she was coming or going. On the morning that the friend was to leave she could barely manage to lay the breakfast table with all the necessary things. Her girlhood friend had to ask for the missing butter, milk and jam. Also, the hostess's little American pill container with the separate sections for each day of the week had suddenly disappeared. No one could understand where the pills had got to. And that morning she left much too little time to get from the house to the airport.

This childhood friendship still somehow belonged to the hostess's old home from their past in another country, before she had got married and had then followed her husband – unnecessarily as it turned out, for later they got separated anyway – to an exile in America.

During their walks and excursions into town and to museums they always returned to the subject of old times. They never tired of this theme. The hostess talked about her old family home, about all the alterations and extensions that had been added, and about how they were now thinking of possibly selling it. 'Oh well, nothing lasts forever,' she comforted herself at the same time. Sometimes the friend regarded her in silence. Perhaps she was thinking: 'Yes, your family home. Yours and mine. Mine and yours. But yours was yours. And mine?'

When they parted at the airport she said: "We'll see each other again!" Then she left and did not once look back. She was the sort of person who does not turn around.

The False Houses

They stayed in front of the glass window for a while, she and her daughter.

Between the two thick panes of glass a big black fly was trapped. It could not get in or out.

Tea in Montparnasse

It is now 1961 and we are in Paris. Every day bombs explode. It is like Belfast later in the nineteen-eighties and beginning of the nineties. And England in 1966. And it was just last Saturday, on June 15th, that the last bomb went off in Manchester. All for nothing. That used to happen constantly in Israel during the governments of Peres and Rabin.

Still, let us return to 1961. My aunt and I were both living in Thiais (Val de Marne). Opposite her house was a large cemetery. It was not until thirty years later that I was to discover that Joseph Roth had been buried there in 1939. His was one of the first graves; the cemetery was opened in 1929. Paul Celan also found his last resting place there in 1970. My aunt (who was not really my aunt, only in this story) now lies in a graveyard too.

Anyway, I will go on with the story, which begins in the nineteen-sixties. My aunt had a little Renault in which we used to drive to town. Later on, I copied her and also bought a small Renault, with a sun roof. One day in Rome, in broad daylight, the car was broken into. I had parked on the Piazza Termini in order to buy some cheap petrol coupons in a shop, but when I came back all the suitcases had disappeared. It was a disaster because I had some valuable things with me and was travelling for three months (Had I forgotten to close the sun roof?)

My aunt had arranged to meet for tea with Uncle Theodore

and Cousin Yvonne (or Denise?) It was not easy to find a parking space so we drove on to the Edgar Quinet Métro station. There we could park opposite another cemetery, Montparnasse. Jean Paul Sartre and Simone de Beauvoir are buried there near the entrance, at the beginning of the path on the right. Once when I was visiting, a woman was standing in front of Sartre's grave, busying herself with pots of flowers and fresh water. While I read the name on the gravestone she introduced herself saying: "I am Mademoiselle Sartre. A distant relative." She looked like an old maid.

"Je suis même partie une fois en Amerique," she told me without being asked. "Bien sur dans un film, quand on a filmé ici."

I said goodbye, for I wanted to visit the grave of Cortázar, who had also been buried there in the meantime. At the beginning of the 1950s, he and I had walked together through this graveyard. That had also been his first time here. He had shown me the grave of Baudelaire, too. I had been told that people bring all sorts of things to Cortazar's grave. That seemed to be true; this time a packet of Gauloises cigarettes lay there. It was seven years after his death in 1984. However, I could not find the grave of César Vallejo; apparently it is somewhat hidden. I laid a few stones on Cortázar's grave according to the Jewish tradition but immediately felt that this was not the right thing to do; it seemed exaggerated. It began to drizzle with rain – now the Gauloises would get wet.

Anyway, my aunt and I strolled down the Boulevard Raspail as far as the statue of Balzac then turned left up the Boulevard Montparnasse. We passed the old Zadkin studio and, lingering in front of various bookshops, continued in the direction of the Avenue de l'Observatoire. At the Closerie de Lilas we stopped and went into the café, which was established in 1803 and had apparently been a favourite haunt of Verlaine's. It is frequently mentioned by Hemingway in his book 'A Moveable Feast', and is often also talked about by Jean Rhys. She once lived near there in the Port Royal area.

Uncle Theodore and Yvonne (or Denise) were sitting in the

garden, or rather, on the terrace, and had saved two places for us. We ordered our tea, spoke about our plans for the summer and of course discussed the current political situation. No day went past without some sort of terrorist attack; everyone kept talking about the attack on de Gaulle in Clamart and so on.

After some time we left, arranging to meet again on the coming Sunday. My aunt and I walked back down the Boulevard Montparnasse but suddenly she stopped, pointing at a suspicious looking package on the ground. "Don't take another step," she said. "We must tell the police." This was quickly done. Immediately a police car drove up and one of the armed policemen approached the package. Passers-by formed a circle and stood around, staring anxiously.

Soon the policeman came back, relieved. Luckily it was not a bomb. It was only some potato peelings wrapped up in brown packing paper, lying right in the middle of the street.

A good excuse for me to tell this story after all these years.

Fine Lace

Cécile was seventeen years old, tall with blonde hair, cornflower blue eyes, slender hands and feet, pretty legs and a light silvery laugh, which sounded like a spring of fresh water. Now she had just fallen in love for the first time in her life. Gaston was eight years older than her, had nearly finished studying German and already had a part-time job. He had left home because he wanted to be independent, and lived in a rented room in one of the many Paris hotels. He was tall and masculine with dark eyes and hair, looked clever, interesting and likeable. But there was something rather inscrutable about his expression, something unfathomable in his handshake. He was very intelligent and alert – a promising, talented young man in every respect. Rumours about his private life circulated among his friends; it had something to do with his having cut himself off from his family at an early age.

Gaston and Cécile got to know each other during the summer holidays in Juan-les-Pins. They went on outings together, talked animatedly for whole afternoons while lying on the beach, and very quickly fell in love with one another. But that summer they did not have intimate relations. Cécile was still a young, inexperienced girl.

Gaston had to leave Juan-les-Pins before she did, writing one delightful letter after another to her from the city. She was more enchanted by each letter, fell more deeply in love and was convinced that once she got back to Paris everything would get even better. She would study the same subject as him and, in time, would leave home, too. Do everything that he did, get to know everything that he knew so that she could get as close as possible to him in every single way.

However, at the end of October when she returned to the city after the long summer vacation, Gaston, despite all his wonderful letters which had sent her into such ecstasies, had all of a sudden changed. Every time they met, he reassured her that he still loved her but she now felt a certain lack of tenderness on his part. She was also surprised by his frequent comments on the way she dressed. He made her get her hair cut very short and forbade her to wear make-up. He wanted her to wear ankle socks instead of elegant silk stockings and look like a little girl, or rather, like a little boy.

Cécile was slightly perturbed by her friend's demands but was still too infatuated to refuse to do what he wanted. On Saturdays and Sundays they would drive in his car out of the city, mostly to the outskirts of Paris to go for a walk. But nowadays she was never alone with him. Gaston always brought some boy from his neighbourhood whom she did not know; they would take photos. Gaston seemed especially to like small boys. Sometimes when they had left Paris he would leave the astounded Cécile sitting by herself in the car while he went for an extra walk on his own with the little boy. Cécile was often surprised by this and sometimes inexplicably jealous.

Gaston had changed so much since that time at the Mediterranean; what was more, he did not want to take her as a woman or make a woman of her. "I have to respect your virginity," he kept repeating, despite the fact that she had got her hair cut so short and made herself look like a little girl just as he wanted her to.

For a long time, nothing changed in their relationship. This situation was making Cécile almost ill. One day, she decided to take things into her own hands and take a gamble. First she moved out of the family home and rented a room in the same hotel as Gaston. She had studied the same subject as him and was now twenty-one years old. She was earning her own living with a part-time job at a bookshop belonging to the father of a friend of Gaston's, so they were seeing each other every day and had got even closer. But he still did not want to make love to her. "It has nothing to do with my feelings for you" he always insisted after every disastrous attempt at physical intimacy. This was beginning to destroy Cécile's sleep and nerves. On Sundays they still usually drove out of town and Gaston always brought some new boy with him. He was especially gifted at making friends with children.

Her laugh had changed, her movements, her posture, her skin, her facial expression. She was no longer happy and seemed terribly troubled by something. She loved Gaston and he did not want to make a woman of her; instead he wanted her to be a little girl.

But one day, five sets of parents stormed into the hotel accompanied by a policeman and demanding to see the owner about one of the guests, a young man whose unlawful behaviour they wanted to report.

Gaston was summoned and asked to admit his wrongdoings. Cécile helped to defend him, saying that the reason for their outings was to take photos. She could prove it, she had always been there with him. Every Sunday, in the car.

Gaston had to pay a large fine and move out of the hotel. He said to Cécile: "Be patient with me; forgive me. You know I love you – I can't help it, one day we will be happy, too."

She was not strong enough to give him up. She was still completely in love with him. And until she found someone better than him, she would not be able to stop loving him. She had tried so often to leave him but just could not manage it. She attempted going out with other men in order to lose her 'innocence'; she thought that if she was more mature as a woman she could perhaps do more for Gaston. But it was all in vain.

Yesterday, I met her again by chance after five years.

"And Gaston . . . ?" I asked.

"He's working for . . ."

Nothing had changed. It reminded me of very fine, valuable lace onto which some acidic fluid had been dripping for years and years, gradually eating up the fabric until it was all yellow and decayed.

Give Yourself a Treat and Go to the Cinema

René Allio had made a film of Bertholt Brecht's short story 'Die unwürdige Greisin' ('The Unworthy Old Woman'). At last the film was due to be shown in Buenos Aires. Sometimes I got the intermediate German class to read the story. In the film version, by the way, the story was set not in Augsburg but in Allio's birthplace in the South of France. Many, many years later, when he visited the Institut Français in London he told me that the old lady in the story was based on his grandmother. In those days (when was it, the end of January 1968?) I could hardly wait for the film to come to Buenos Aires, and went to the premiere. As always, whenever possible, I sat in the eighth row. I knew the cinema from many years back. It was called 'The Libertador', like the wide, elegant avenue in town, Avenida Libertador, which was modelled on London's Park Lane. Along one side of it were houses, on the other a beautiful park. The cinema, like the avenue, was named Libertador after San Martin. This highly honoured general and politician was born in 1778 in Yapeyú, in the province of Correntes. Around 1821 he had liberated Argentina, Chile and Peru (all three in one go) from the Spanish. There are statues of San Martin in all these countries;

streets and squares are named after him and he is celebrated as a national hero. Later in his life, disgusted by the squabbling and infighting of rivals, he left Argentina and went to London where he lived at first for a while in a house opposite Regents Park in Park Road. Later he moved to Boulogne-sur-Mer in France where he died in 1850.

The Libertador Cinema had always specialised in French films. The Cine Luxor used to and still does show German films. As soon as the French weekly Pathé news show with its signature tune and spinning cockerel had ended, the cinema house lights went up for a few minutes. I turned round and noticed a face a few rows behind me which I somehow recognised. At first I could not think who it was, for I had been away from Buenos Aires again for a few years. But next to this masculine face sat a woman, still blonde despite being in her seventies, with untidy, carelessly combed hair. My God, those are the Gompertzs. The parents of an old school friend of mine called Susie, who often used to visit us when my mother was still running the large guest house. My mother always used to complain about her because she ate up all the sugar, lump by lump. She probably did not get enough to eat at home and was just hungry. Actually the Gompertz family was not doing so badly in those days. That was during the first wave of emigration; war had not yet broken out in Germany but, all the same, they had left in 1936, already because of Hitler. In Hanover, where they had lived, they had been a well-off middle class family. The mother came from the beautiful town of Hildesheim and they all spoke very cultured German compared to that of other German emigrants. Moreover, the mother had a wonderful way with us teenage girls. She was very understanding and had a good sense of humour. She called me 'the pocket-sized adventurer' because I always used to tell new, strange stories. When, at the age of thirteen or fourteen we reached the next stage of physical maturity, it was she who found a word for it: 'Boom-boom'. "Susie is already boom-boom, are you too, Gertrude?" This expression stuck with us and even years later we would write it in our diaries around the same day of every month. Later, when our own children had reached this stage, we passed the expression on to them.

As a child, Susie had started having ballet lessons in Hanover with Curt Joos. One day he came to Buenos Aires with his ballet company. We especially admired their performance of 'The Green Table'. Susie danced to the music of one of Chopin's Impromptus at our school-leaving celebration. She often wrote in her diary: 'I can only express my joys and sorrows through dance.' Susie was nice really, but, from her early years, based her friendships on what she could gain from them. She was always more impressed by friends from rich families than by those from poor ones. We others were much too naive for the schemes and ideas which she came up with. For example, we three girls had five centavos between us and wanted to buy six sweets. Each cost one centavo. Then Susie said to the man behind the counter in the sweet shop: "How much is that packet of biscuits up there?" and the minute the man turned round to reach up for the biscuits she quickly snatched another sweet. So we had six sweets and got two each. Or another example: the three of us used to catch the train to school from Retiro station to Belgrano R., for we all lived in the centre of town. We often jumped into the train at the last minute and then had to walk through the first class carriage into the second class. Susie always made sure she was the one in the middle; once she admitted proudly that it was so that she would not have to open or close any of the connecting doors. That would never have occurred to us.

Fate was to dictate that Susie would marry a playboy from a rich family, bringing five girls into the world. In the end she had to go to work because of their financial problems. But until now I have not mentioned Susie's brother Jochen, and actually this story was meant to be about him – in fact, I'm only writing this all down because of him. Jochen was about four years older than Susie. Medium-sized, narrow brown eyes, a long nose, sensual lips, a high forehead, dark hair. He wore rimless spectacles and looked rather like a chemistry student or pharmacist. "If we had stayed in Germany, I would have studied medicine," he always used to say.

All Susie's friends were in love with Jochen for a while but he only fell for Irene, who became his girlfriend for several years but whom he did not want to marry. It was Irene's first experience of love and this was a hard blow for her. After that she married an older, not good-looking but very rich man just to please her parents. So she became a not very happy but at least a very rich woman.

When the Boogie-woogie came into fashion and we ex-pupils from the same school used to go dancing together once a week, Jochen lectured me: "You can't just fling yourself around like that" and as to the others his comment was: "All hopeless cases."

At the age of twenty-three or twenty-four, Jochen thought it would be better to leave home and live alone in a bachelor pad. He was working for his father in an import/export business. It was right next to the old department of philosophy, Viamonte 416, and I passed it every day on my way to the office. I remember a wonderful autumn morning in September 1939; I was going past the office when Jochen called me in to show me the headlines of a morning newspaper in heavy print: war had broken out in Europe.

After that I did not see him for years. The last I heard of him, before I finally left for Europe, was that he had found the woman of his life and was very happy. She was no fashion queen but very intelligent and they were made for each other – in their free time they even played chess with each other. They had three children, all girls.

When, after twelve years, I came back on a visit to Buenos Aires, my cousin told me that she often saw Jochen Gompertz and that their children got on well together. Jochen was keen to see me again. Although he had separated from his wife in the meantime, they were still good friends. "Yes, of course," I said to her, "tell him to give me a ring – give him my number."

One summer evening he came to pick me up and we drove in

his car along the Avenida Libertador. He pointed out the dancers in a neon-light advertisement for Argentinian Champagne, 'Duc du Saint Rémy'.

"My children really love those dancers," he said "and I must admit, it's a really attractive advertisement – I show it to all the tourists who come to Buenos Aires."

We ate Argentine steak and salad in a nice restaurant on the Rio de la Plata (without getting plagued by mosquitos). Jochen was on good form although somewhat nervous and embarrassed. He kept dropping things, first the car key with which he could not stop playing around, then the cigarettes and then the lighter.

"You have changed for the better," he said more than once. We spoke about school friends whom we remembered from the past. He said that materially he was the worst off of all of them.

"If only I could have studied, my life would have been much more interesting," he kept lamenting.

"If you had really wanted to study, wouldn't it have been possible?" I interjected. "Lots of people work and study at the same time, especially in this country. The studies just take longer."

"Easier said than done," he replied. At that time he was an Anthroposophist and belonged to the Rudolf Steiner circle in Buenos Aires.

There was no particular reason for the break-up of his marriage. Most likely was that she was more intelligent than him and that his problems with his own character led him to destroy everything around him. A real personality problem.

His wife lived out of town in a small villa with a garden, in the suburb of Martinez, thirty minutes by train from the town centre. Jochen had moved into a bachelor pad again, in the middle of town. He paid for the monthly upkeep of his family and visited his children regularly. He had given his wife a small Fiat. But one day she had a car accident on the lovely wide Avenida Libertador, right opposite the lit-up advertisement for Duc du Remy with the dancers. She was immediately taken to hospital where she lay unconscious being artificially fed by drip. After three months she died without once having regained consciousness. The three girls were eight, ten and twelve years old. Jochen gave up his bachelor pad and moved back to his children in the old family home.

I returned to Europe, and one day my mother wrote to me that Jochen had remarried, a divorcee or widow who also had three children and that they were all living together in the house in Martinez.

After some time my mother mentioned in her letters that this second marriage of Jochen's had not worked either and that, although still good friends, they were living separately.

In one of the next letters was the death announcement of Jochen. A heart attack at the age of forty-two.

In his will he assigned the upbringing of the children to some old school friends, who did indeed take the children in.

A few days after his death, his parents found out that he had bankrupted the firm. He had got into such terrible debt during the last few years and had so completely lost his bearings that he could see no way out. His parents, who were over seventy years old, had everything taken from them – every single valuable thing in the house, such as pictures, silver and so on.

They moved to a two-roomed flat and kept their heads above water thanks to a monthly cheque in dollars which was sent by a generous cousin in Canada. Should the cousin die before them, my mother said, they just did not know how they would survive. They never visited the cemetery – they did not believe in that.

She told me all this later in the small café. As to whether Susie could help them, the answer was no. Apart from anything else, her husband suffered from paranoia and was always frightened that he would get sent to prison. And the family doctor, Dr Elias, who was a friend of theirs, wrote on the death certificate that Jochen had officially died of a heart attack although it was, of course, suicide.

After the film had finished we found ourselves standing opposite one another in the cinema foyer. I greeted them first and they recognised me. She still had large, round and expressive blue eyes.

Her hair had stayed naturally ash blonde and was not dyed. The colour of her arms was still very white and she had remained, just as before, the nice lady still with the beautiful German accent. What had happened to her was terrible, more than terrible, yet she had kept her poise. Her husband had large bags under his eyes and a somewhat bleary expression.

"What did you think of the film?" I asked.

"Wonderful! I know Brecht's short stories," she said. "My husband had a good sleep in the cinema of course. Magnificent, Sylvie's interpretation of 'Die unwürdige Greisin'. No wonder she got the French Academy and Festival of Rio de Janeiro prizes for the best interpretation of the year."

'How well informed she is.' I thought. 'She appears to be one of those unshakeable, steadfast types.'

"So you see, Karoline, this is what is left for us. We spend a few enjoyable hours going to the cinema."

The Au Pair

"I can't use you like a donkey on your very first day," said the lady, as they returned from the market and slowly climbed the steep Nadelberg Strasse up to the lady's flat on the third or fourth floor of an old house. This house had been renovated but, many years later, it was to burn down.

The flat was on the small side, but pretty. In the entrance hall was enough space for a coat stand on which the lady's Cocteau coat (a coat with a hood) hung – fashionable in the fifties, and nowadays she used it both as a coat and as a dressing-gown. Next to it stood a little table on which always lay three small balls, red, green and blue. Once the girl put the red ball in between the blue and green ones. "Oh no, that won't do," said the lady, "the blue ball must always go next to the green or the green next to the blue one, those are the rules."

On the right was the door to the lady's room. The room in which she lived and worked. High up on the wall hung a reproduction of 'Nike of Samothrake', the fourth century BC original of which was in the Louvre in Paris.

Of course, there was also a gramophone and in the mornings music could be heard coming from her room. Mostly, it was Beethoven's Egmont Overture. There were two more doors in the hall; one led to the bathroom and the other to the spacious kitchen which doubled as a living-room. On the left-hand side was one more, very beautiful, room with light pouring through a large window. That was used as a study or guest room, and it was there that the girl now lived.

In Paris the lady had said to the girl: "Come and stay with me for a few weeks in Switzerland. I can show you how to work more quickly. I won't be so alone then and I'll have some help in the house. Nowadays young people are left so much to their own devices. You're a generation younger than I am. When I was studying, everything was different; we were a community. There was really close contact between students and their teachers."

And often, during or after breakfast, she told stories about her youth and about what one used to wear in those days. Her description of a bodice with countless little buttons, which she had once owned, was so vivid that the girl could almost see her sitting there in just that bodice. And she talked about how her teachers in those days took young people seriously. And that someone had said to her: " 'You can do anything.' Just imagine what it's like if someone says that to a young person. That stayed with me for my whole life." Abruptly she broke off, looked into the girl's eyes and said: "I find you too weak!"

On another occasion she talked about the time after the Second World War when she had stayed behind on her own in New York and had been obliged to earn her own living. Her husband, from whom she was now separated (he was in Paris and she in Switzerland, though they were still good friends and in regular contact) had gone off back to France straight after the war with an eighteen year-old girl. "I felt very bitter about that in those days," she said. It was not until a few months later that his conscience got the better of him and he sent her the money for a ticket home.

"The only thing I had in those days, and still do have, was and is my German language. Sometimes I have even spoken German to the walls," she said. Now she was working successfully as a translator. Her husband was able to send her a lot of material from Paris. "I don't mind living alone so much any more. That's how I was able to find myself again," she said sometimes.

She also talked about Simone de Beauvoir, who, when Sartre moved in with another woman, at first wanted to take her own life.

And it was that which somehow linked the girl to the lady, consciously or unconsciously. A woman's similar fate which they had in common although the girl was a generation younger.

Sometimes in the late afternoon they would go for a walk by the Rhine, and the lady told the girl that when she first lived here, she used to come down to the Rhine after a day of solid and concentrated work, and would sit on a bench on the river bank and smoke a cigarette. In those days it was all she could afford.

In the meantime she had also taught the girl how to prepare proper Swiss muesli. There was always some on the breakfast table. One day she said: "Now go and try to translate the first page of that story. There's a typewriter in your room and you'll find a dictionary in there too." She was referring to the manuscript of a story told in a foreign language, twelve pages long, which the girl had brought with her. Her friend in Paris had given her permission to translate it; it was not yet published in his own language.

The girl did this and enjoyed herself; she did not find it very difficult. Before lunch she brought the first finished page to the lady's room. Soon after, the lady appeared as always for lunch in the kitchen but this time she was waving the page in her hand.

"Good news!" she said. "YOU CAN DO IT!"

The Second Visit or
Lotte in London

Twenty-five years ago they turned up for the first time. In those days we were still living in the first flat that we had in London. It was near Swiss Cottage in the north of the city. The flat was called, somewhat grandly, a 'garden flat'. In German it would have merely been called a basement flat, although it did have direct access to the garden. After all, a basement flat like that has to have at least one good thing about it. The garden was large and more or less square in shape. They had to share it with the other tenants in the house, though. On the ground floor lived Mr. Whiting, who paid less rent in return for acting as caretaker. Mr. Whiting shared his surname with the playwright John Whiting, whose play 'The Devils', inspired by the true story of what happened in Poitiers in the sixteenth century, had been so successful in the sixties. The Mr. Whiting living in this house had actually been an actor, but not a particularly successful one; nowadays he just wrote some short texts called 'features' for the BBC. I often saw him going to the letterbox on the corner of Strathray Gardens and Eton Avenue and dropping his daily post into those round, red English pillar boxes of medium height, which can also be found in Portugal and Argentina. Cortázar mentions them in his book 'The

Winners' and compares them to the back view of a slim lady in long red trousers. Apparently there are similar post boxes in Ireland, only they are green like everything else there. I once dreamt that I saw my German grandmother standing by the letterbox at that particular corner. Her hair was hanging down loose over her shoulders and was completely white. Of course she had died long before, but she seemed to be trying to tell me something. And in a way, this story is perhaps a letter to her. Or perhaps, by appearing to me in a dream, she wanted me to know that from now on I should never stop writing to her.

In the garden there were blackberries which tasted wonderfully sweet. Also living in the house was an elderly German couple who kept having terribly loud arguments. The wife had been born and brought up in Berlin but had left with her husband because of the race laws. The fragments of German which one heard were anything but complimentary.

The second floor was occupied temporarily by Chileans – an academic with his family who had left Santiago because of the military rule there. That had been at the beginning of the seventies, when so many of his compatriots had been forced to leave their country.

"The climate over there was never a problem," he said, "but when one has always taken sunshine for granted, the English weather is nearly unbearable. And we hardly ever buy meat here; the cost is prohibitive."

The owner of the house was an English Jew of Russian descent. He owned another house further up on the same street. On the first or last day of every month he always rang up punctually to ask for the rent. That seemed to be his main income. When we moved in, he surprised us by suddenly saying: "Mazel Tov!" (That means: 'Good Luck') And I was once told by one of the tenants from the other house that whenever this landlord came to her flat he would sit down at her piano and quickly play a Scarlatti sonata. He claimed to have been a concert pianist once. So it was to this so-called furnished 'garden flat' that the visitor came for the first time.

But now, twenty-five years later, things were quite different. It was another flat. And our family circumstances had changed. This time, the visitor came to do an official interview, with a cameraman in tow. She had found out that her one-time acquaintance had been the inspiration for an important character in a world-famous novel by an author from the same country. This author would have been eighty years old this year had he lived, but he had died ten years before, and was now greatly honoured and celebrated in her country.

Four of them came and stayed in a hotel near her flat. In their country in the other part of the world, they had studied the map of London and thoroughly prepared everything for their stay. The so-called friend doing the interview was allowed to bring along her husband as a bonus, not to mention a man from the banking foundation which was financing the whole project and paying all the bills; also present was the son of the bank director who was doing something in the film world.

On the first day, two of the men travelled to Cambridge specifically to hire a camera. The next time they all met was in the hotel, where plans for the coming days were discussed. It was one of those typical tourist hotels used by charter companies, near Oxford Street and Marble Arch. An escalator led up to the reception area where a mammoth grand piano, looking rather like a bull, played continuous melodies all by itself without any human hands. She associated this monster of an instrument with the whole nature of the visit. Why, she could not quite explain to herself. It was as though she were seeing these people for the first time. After all, twenty-five years is a long time, a notable sort of anniversary. First of all they searched for a café. The conversation was all about the deceased author. Sentences were seemingly tossed casually into the conversation – she only realised later that they were actually carefully aimed. Then they were joined by the other two men who said how glad they were to meet her and touched her as if she were a valuable object.

The next day the camera was set up in her flat and the so-called interview began. The lady interviewer turned up wearing what she evidently considered an elegant blouse with three different necklaces around her neck – a style apparently still in fashion in that other part of the world. The camera man said: "You have to wear either a black or a white blouse."

In her own flat, they were the ones who chose a chair and a corner for her to sit in. When the dialogue began she did not notice that they avoided using her surname. That only struck her much later. "Where did you see him for the first time?" The interviewer used her Christian name; in her country it was normal to be on familiar terms almost immediately. For the rest of the questions she relied on a few typewritten sheets, written, signed and sent previously to the other country by the interviewee. Coming to England and filming was actually completely superfluous. But the journey to Europe was all paid for, so why not? After about one hour, the camera man said: "Now it's my turn to ask a question: do you still dream about him – I mean, do you still love him?" Astonished by this question, her brief answer was "No!" Then he wanted to see her old photos, which she kept in an old envelope. They sorted through them and chose some photos of her old aunts and other members of her family. They pinned them onto a wooden board, together with an old handkerchief from her childhood which also happened to be in the envelope, then photographed and filmed the whole board. 'What a strange invasion of my home!' she thought to herself every now and then.

"Right, let's all go and have some supper now," said the man from the banking foundation. She suggested a nearby Italian restaurant, La Fontana Amorosa in Blenheim Crescent. Meanwhile they had filmed her house from the outside as well as the EMI studios opposite, which were made famous by The Beatles in the sixties. In the restaurant later on, the young camera man, who was a bit too well fed and looked like a typical Daddy's boy, kept fondling her back. Late that evening he rang her up from his hotel and told her something that she could hardly believe: the next day he was travelling to Mexico where he wanted to gather even more film material, all for the memorial festival taking place in the capital city of her country.

The man who signed all the bills was going on to Paris. The 'visitor' who had set all this up was going to stay on in London for a whole week – after all, it would not cost her anything. Then she would follow the banker to Paris.

Despite these enormous outgoings, the 'contact' herself was not offered a cent. 'Are they really so stupid and uneducated or just incredibly rude?' she wondered. And she named a price equivalent to the hire of the camera just for one day. Embarrassed, they replied: "Yes, yes of course – we can't arrange it right now but we'll do it when we get home." The finance man repeated this three or four times, until she began to feel almost suspicious. Then the visitors left for Paris, where they had booked a hotel for another week.

Two months later, an article appeared in the Sunday supplement of an important newspaper in her country bearing the title: 'Lotte in London.' An entirely fictitious interview with manipulated facts from the article which she herself had originally sent them.

'I hope you don't mind' wrote the interviewer, 'I didn't mention your name as you didn't want to be identified with the main character in the novel. Anyway, for me it was a huge success.'

Elvira in the Big City

By chance, Elvira had landed up in the Hotel de la Vieille Église. She had left home and decided to take her life into her own hands, living in a city and doing some sort of work that suited her. It just had to work out, she had to make it a success, even if it meant going without many things.

The hotel was in a very beautiful part of Paris; the first time she entered it she saw a woman standing in the entrance hall, whose face she found interesting yet at the same time vaguely irritating. The woman's smile, which was rather veiled, gave nothing away. She did not realise that this woman was to influence her destiny in this city.

She was given a nice room on the top floor of the building with a built-in kitchen, or rather, a kitchenette. The hotel was called Vieille Église after the oldest church in Paris, built in the twelfth century, which lay almost opposite, just five hundred metres away. The hotel was surrounded by an old, very pretty park and on the terrace was a simple café. For years it had been popular among journalists, actors, photographers and people who either wrote or wanted to write. The owners were proud of its prestigious reputation. They said: "Everyone who lived here made their way in the world. We never had Bohemians living here." And they reeled off a list of artists who were indeed famous. It was hard to tell what made this hotel so special – whether it was the pleasant atmosphere or the peaceful setting.

Elvira soon got to know several interesting people living in this building. One of them was Madame Koza, or Ina Bandy, a photographer of Russian descent – actually a Russian who had lived in France since the revolution. She was the oldest guest and had lived in the hotel for over twelve years, since her divorce. She occupied two rooms: one at the back, which she used as a studio and darkroom, and one at the front with a direct view onto the Seine and the wonderful trees which had, during all the years with their many seasons, become almost like family to her. This room had a kitchenette. Elvira was full of admiration for Madame Koza, who was perhaps fifty-three years old. Her photos were excellent. She mostly took photos of works of art – pictures in exhibitions – and she travelled to all sorts of galleries and museums both in France and abroad. Her work had prestige; she was a renowned photographer and could live off her work. Other subjects of hers were based on well-known themes from the works of Van Gogh or Cézanne.

For these she would travel to the places where the pictures had originally been painted. Sometimes she would invite the young acolytes, who often sat observing her at work in her studio, to accompany her on her travels and this was how it came about that one day she invited Elvira to go with her to

Auvers- sur-Oise.

Elvira could draw and paint a little. She did not get on well with her parents and found life in the provinces boring. Her parents had refused to support her financially, even for just the beginning of her studies. Her father thought that there was no need for her to go away; she would be much better off staying in the small town where she could help him in the bakery – and, anyway, she was bound to get married later.

Elvira's pride was wounded and her feelings were hurt. 'I'll show them' she said to herself. This little town was not her whole world – now she was going to fight her own way through life.

She wanted to learn to paint properly, which meant going to a good art college, and she would find some way of earning enough money to live on.

Before she left, she went to the office of the small local newspaper, where she had already earned a bit of pocket money by illustrating some stories. There she asked if she could go on sending them illustrations, but now from the capital city. The sub-editor nodded in a friendly fashion, agreeing to her suggestion and even said: "Yes, of course – and send us a report about this or that exhibition every now and then, too." So Elvira, armed with her small savings, travelled happily and optimistically to Paris.

She had been lucky to find the room in the Hotel de la Vielle Église and she felt at home there. Immediately she enrolled in an art academy, visited museums and exhibitions, and spent some happy weeks getting to know many young people with whom, for the first time in her young life, she could speak about things that interested her. Was it really possible that life could be so wonderful?

Everything was going very well for her except for one worry which was so great that it even worked its way into her dreams: she was getting short of money. Although she did receive some payment by post every now and then for her illustrations and reports for the local newspaper back home, it was not enough to live on. The rent was due. She started worrying about what to do. She tried selling her illustrations to other newspapers, but soon the situation became so acute that she was forced to borrow money to pay the rent at least. It was out of the question that the hotel owner should find out that she was in trouble or she would immediately forfeit her nice room. She borrowed some money from her new friends and did not yet know how she would repay them; but she knew that she would manage it, somehow. She also borrowed fifty old francs from Madame Koza, the understanding and independent woman whom she admired so much. For the time being, she did not want even to consider taking on a job in a shop or an office – she was frightened that she would not be able to attend art college any more, would have to give up her ideals and that her father would be proved right after all. She was in complete despair about this lack of money. She had got into more debt and could not always pay the money back on time. Her friends understood and said that they did not mind; they sympathised with how it felt, and they also knew that she would pay them back as soon as she was in a position to do so. Only Madame Koza smiled mysteriously and said: "You remind me of someone…"

By chance, the editor of her hometown newspaper set up a contact for her with a lady who also painted and illustrated and who would be staying in the same hotel for the next few days. This lady actually lived in the French part of Switzerland and had got to know the editor at a conference of journalists shortly before her journey to Paris. She had given him her address in Paris. The editor noticed that it was the same hotel as that in which the baker's daughter was living; subconsciously he was worried about her. "Please, do look out for this young girl," he asked Madame Sufflot.

When she arrived in Paris, Madame Sufflot had the girl called to her room. Elvira was very impressed by this wonderful woman's personality and thought to herself: 'She's sure to understand that I'm searching for a really serious meaning in my life and perhaps she will help me on my way.' They liked each other. Madame Sufflot told Elvira something of her life story. About her husband, who was French and had abandoned her in America after the Second World War; although they had been through thick and thin together (she was German) he had simply upped and left with an eighteen-year-old girl – despite the fact that when he was a prisoner of war in Tunisia she had cooked soup for him every day, on a fire made of a few paltry sticks, and walked two kilometres to bring it to him. All that she told Elvira the very first time they met. In those days in America, she said, when she was all on her own, she also just had to find a way of surviving somehow. She, too, had done illustrations for newspapers but had been through hard, hard times and could understand only too well.

While she was talking, someone knocked at the door. It was Madame Koza and it turned out that the women were girlhood friends. Elvira took her leave at once. As she was going, Madame Sufflot called to her that she would leave a note in her key pigeon-hole downstairs to say at what time they could meet the next day. Madame Kutya Koza watched her quizzically as she left the room.

Elvira skipped up the stairs happily to her room. She had the feeling that now a new door had opened for her and that with the understanding and help of this wonderful woman, sent to her by fate, she would manage to find the right path through life.

As soon as they were alone, Madame Koza attacked her old friend with the question: "How do you know that girl?" Madame Sufflot explained how the introduction had come about.

"Watch out," said Madame Koza. "She's bound to ask you for money, she is a scrounger and already owes money to all sorts of people".

"You're mad, Kutya," replied Ely Sufflot. "She's got into difficulties, that's all. Weren't we both in the same situation once? She made a good impression on me – you shouldn't always think the worst of people straight away."

"Well, anyway," said Kutya Koza. "She has owed me five hundred old francs for one and a half months now. She keeps putting me off from one week to the next. She'll never pay me back. My husband – as you know, we separated twelve years ago- was just the same. He used the same excuse as her to borrow from my mother and all my best friends, one after the other."

"But Kutya, there's simply no comparison."

Ely Sufflot knew that life had not been kind to Kutya Koza. Although she was a good and successful photographer, she was mistrustful and fearful of others; she lived a very lonely life in this hotel.

Ely Sufflot still felt a certain sympathy for this old friend and used to meet up for a drink with her whenever she came to Paris. They had both suffered a similar fate. She too had lost her husband to another woman and, because of this, lived in a different country, although she was not isolated like Madame Koza. She had also had many ugly experiences and had sometimes been mistaken about other people's characters. But her heart and mind told her that this young girl was not a reckless scrounger.

The next day, as arranged, she put a little note in Elvira's pigeonhole, saying that she would be waiting for her in her room at seven o'clock. She would prepare a small supper. Elvira was thrilled by this news and that evening at seven she knocked at the door, holding a single rose as a little present. Madame Sufflot was staying in one of the hotel rooms looking directly onto the Seine, while Elvira, as a monthly paying guest, lived in a smaller room. They talked about this and that and Elvira, thinking to herself that this generous lady would surely understand her money problems, soon asked her to lend her one hundred new (or, as it was in those days, ten thousand old) francs. Her rent was nine thousand francs. She would pay her back in two months' time. The rent was due and she simply did not know how to pay it. The landlady must not find out about her present difficulties, otherwise she would lose her room.

Despite Madame Koza's warning, Ely Sufflot immediately agreed. At the moment she could easily help her out with the hundred new francs for two months. She did not believe in Kutya's cautionary remarks. She just thought that this child had lost her way, simply because she was not yet capable of working with discipline in the right way.

"Alright, Elvira," she said, handing her the hundred francs. "Try to keep going for a while here in this city and if you can't manage, come and stay with me in Switzerland. We'll work together and I'll help you to go further on the path which you've chosen."

As well as the money, Madame Sufflot gave her a Neapolitan filter coffee pot which stood on the table, and which had impressed Elvira a lot.

"Here you are," she said. "If one lives in a hotel one should at least have good coffee. I know what it's like. I belong to that generation of Germans who have always lived a lot in hotels and it's always important to have a little portable coffee maker and a small camping gas stove. If you put several teaspoonfuls of coffee into the filter you can even make mocha."

Elvira, made deeply happy by this spontaneous gesture, kept this type of coffee-maker forever after. In all the countries in which she later lived, she always managed to find a shop where one could replace it two or three times a year. Later in her life, when she visited this same lady, who was now living out her old age in Paris, she told her about this tradition with the Neapolitan coffee-maker which she had kept up her whole life. The old lady could not remember it any more and said: "Nowadays I use a thermos flask; it keeps the coffee hot for a long time. And" she added, referring to the one on the table and laughing, "you're not getting this one!"

Two months later Elvira travelled to Ely Sufflot's house in Switzerland and lived there for a while as an au pair

Some months later she returned to Paris, with greatly increased courage and self-confidence.

The Tiled Stove

In November 1959 my newspaper sent me to the Maison de France in Berlin to attend the lecture by Alain Robbe-Grillet about the new way of novel-writing in France. Next to me in the conference room sat a young woman who caught my eye. I noticed immediately that she resembled me in many ways. Later, at the cocktail reception, we started a conversation. She was working at a publisher's, had been a widow for some years – her husband had died in the war – and was now living alone. Afterwards we had had a drink in the elegant restaurant upstairs, to which only foreigners or guests of foreigners had access, I gave her a lift home in my little Renault.

At that time, my life, including my love life, was rather turbulent. One day, when all this was behind me, as I was already comforting myself, I would ring this young woman, which would mean in effect that I had returned to my former life as a single woman.

As it happened, by Christmas things had been decided – more or less. The man was spending Christmas Eve with his family.

I rang Irmgard Kluse and we arranged to meet. I knew she would understand my problem and immediately told her the whole story. She just said: "Come to my house tomorrow afternoon around 5 o'clock; later, when my mother and brother turn up for Christmas Eve, you'll be free and can do whatever you like." My presents from her were a paperback edition of German poetry and a small, rather kitschy, and very German candle holder and a candle to go with it. All I had with me was Robbe-Grillet's latest book 'Jalousie', just published, a book that I had not read yet myself. I left it with her as a present.

Two years later I came back to Berlin and said 'Hallo' to Irmgard Kruse, among others. I had sent her a postcard from the other continent. She was pleased to see me again and spontaneously invited me to stay with her for a few days. I accepted, and the first five days were truly nice. At all costs, I also wanted to meet up again with my former friend. I had found out that, for the past four months, he had been living alone, or rather dossing down, in some sort of a hall, somewhat hidden and yet in the centre of town on the Kurfürstendamm. He reckoned that there at last he had enough space to paint his large pictures, although the conditions there were extremely basic. There was neither electricity nor any heating facility. From November onwards, he had no light after about 4 o'clock. His wife was living in their flat as before and now and again wondered whether he might not fall ill in his so-called studio. She did understand, though, that he needed this large space for his work.

Friends gave me his address, and one Saturday afternoon I knocked on his door. By then it was 6 o'clock and he was sitting, huddled, in the freezing place. A woollen blanket was draped across his back and beneath that he was also wearing three thick sweaters. And all this by candlelight.

He was greatly surprised to see me, but was just as pleased as I was. Both of us were a little embarrassed and didn't quite know what to say. Something about the past, about which we both felt awkward – although we had not forgotten the wonderful time we had spent together, brief though it had been.

I told him: "I am staying at a friend's, not far from here, come with me so that you can warm up a little. She has a marvellous tiled stove, and you can have supper with us, and we can listen to some music as well."

When he heard this he smiled, but I did not like this smile very much. I could not say why I didn't. He came along without further ado.

I introduced him to Irmgard and he liked her at first glance. We first served him some hot soup. He immediately took off his third, and warmest, sweater and would not stop looking at the tiled stove which he admired and which apparently reminded him of his grandmother. She had, so he told us, had one just like it in Bitterfeld; a white cat had always sat underneath it, and he now quite expected to see a paw or her tail looking out from under the stove.

In her library he spotted a book with good coloured prints of pictures by Cezanne, whom he adored, as well as some by Sam Francis and Ernst-Wilhelm Nay.

After supper, we put on some records. They were nearly all the same ones as those that I had had two years earlier. The only one missing was Edith Piaf's 'Tu me fais tourner la tête'. Instead of that, however, she had Piaf's 'Avant nous' and 'Les amants d'un jour'. We avoided eye contact. After that we listened to some jolly Spanish music which Irmgard had brought back from her trip to Spain, and later still she put on some classical music. The friend said that the evening had been wonderful. He had been feeling a great hunger to spend a few civilised hours. At around 11.30 I took him to the front door. To make things simpler, I quickly put on Irmgard's elegant winter coat which was hanging in the hall. That earned me a compliment from him. The three minutes we then spent alone together made us feel rather awkward. We had nothing more to say to each other, absolutely nothing.

"Do look in again some time," he called out to me as he was leaving.

"Thank you," I replied and disappeared back into the house.

Visiting the Green House

"I'll get your coat for you," she said and, disappearing for a second, went up four or five stairs to where there seemed to be a small coat stand. At least, there were several hooks on the wall where visitors could hang their coats. Perhaps some of them did hang their jackets and coats there. Simply a place to hang coats like nearly everybody had in their houses.

Now, the house. The house. The outside was still painted green. A peculiar shade of green. Neither olive nor light or even a proper green. More an indefinable, neither beautiful nor particularly striking green. The other houses in this rather short street were white. Perhaps there was one light blue one among them diagonally opposite. If she ever returned to the area she ought to have a look.

But actually, it is more important to talk about the interior of the house or, rather, the person who lives there.

As her taxi turned into the street on that particular evening she could already see from the distance two large illuminated windows on the top floor. This time, someone was waiting for her. There was even supper prepared for her in the spacious kitchen although they had actually planned to go out for dinner. "I'm not going out," said the lady of the house, and that suited the visitor. It was a very cold evening on that first day of March in 1993.

She rang the bell briefly and spoke her name into the entry

phone. Straightaway the lady came downstairs and opened the door leading to the first floor. Downstairs on the ground floor were two rooms, right and left, which she sometimes rented out or, if she needed to, she used them herself. When our visitor was new to this country, she had lived in the room on the right. But that had been twenty-four years ago. Now, as she entered the house, the rooms lay in darkness.

Upstairs, by better light, she looked at the lady's face. She now had white hair and had aged quite naturally. The visitor was surprised to see that she looked like her mother's sister, Aunt Gustel, known more formally as Aunt Augusta. She was the one in the family who had done best in life; as a young girl she had apparently been very beautiful and had had one admirer after another. Her hair was black and her eyes blue. She had also cherished certain ideals and once admitted to her niece that she did not identify with her children. When I related that to my mother she was rather pleased. "Did she really say that?" she often repeated. I wonder if my mother, who died a long time ago, identified at least partly with me.

"I gained nothing at all from your youth," she once reproached me. I had left her alone for too long and gone off to a distant country, always landing up in the wrong houses there.

"You look young," said my hostess. Well, I did indeed look young. My hair still had not started to go grey and I had a young hairstyle. And that evening I was wearing my red scarf as I sometimes did when I needed extra confidence. I was also planning to buy myself a red cashmere scarf in the sales. It would have to be a particular, very beautiful pale red which suited me.

So now we sat opposite one another at supper. Her manner of scrutinising me was strange for me. I cannot remember how I reacted but I am sure it was with an instinctively defensive reserve. The food tasted good and the guest or, rather I myself, mentioned that I had not forgotten the Chinese dish recipe; I would like to taste it again and also the Swabian potato salad with onions. She smiled, evidently pleased with that comment. Then we talked a little about plays and films. She said that she worked forty hours a week.

"Have you got so many patients?"

"Partly students too."

On the table lay a book on psychoanalysis. She had found her way into this second profession over the years; it seemed to give her a certain satisfaction and kept her busy.

Later we went into the room opposite, her sitting room, which she still used as a study. On the wall were various family photos. Her father, mother, grandparents. I forgot to ask whether they were on her father's or mother's side. They hung one above the other, like Chinese or Japanese script. I, the guest, remarked that she must have spoken in a nice Swabian dialect and again saw a smile flit across her face. Then I sat down on a chair which was rather too low and suddenly, in the middle of the conversation, got cramp in my left thigh. I had never had cramp there before. I stood up, trying to get rid of it.

"If you're going to stand, then I will too," said the hostess unexpectedly. After a few minutes the cramp had gone but the guest did not want to sit down again.

"Can I sit on this chair, please?" and she pointed to the higher office chair; somewhat surprised, the hostess agreed. On the chair was a handbag which the guest placed on the writing desk.

"You always have small desks," she said.

"Yes," answered the other, "I don't need a large writing desk." Then she added: "I'll get your coat," and brought it to her. The guest put it on straightaway and the hostess said: "Here's your handbag!"

"No, this one's mine," said the guest and took it from the armchair.

"It looks just like mine, I've had it for fifteen years," said the hostess.

Now the guest was ready to leave and her farewell was not as warm as her greeting had been. The hostess proffered her cheek as if to say: 'You may kiss me goodbye.' Years ago, the guest had noticed this habit of hers. And had then used this gesture herself once when visiting an old, somewhat inhibited, friend in Paris for the first time in years; he had immediately reacted in a grateful fashion.

The hostess accompanied her halfway down the steps on which, as she related, she had broken her leg the year before and had had to use crutches for some time. When she came to the word 'crutches' she glanced up but the other was not impressed and did not return her look. Now she had completely recovered from the accident. The corners of her mouth turned down a little. Though hardly. And after all, she had been through a lot, the hostess.

"See you next time," said the guest, already on the street. The hostess gave her a final, rather veiled look.

She walked down the short street to the corner with the house where, according to the blue plaque, Friedrich Engels had lived from 1870-1894. Along came a taxi and five minutes later she was home. Even while still unlocking her front door, she had already forgotten her visit to the green house.

The Ceremonial Sword

Every day in his lunch break, the twenty-five-year-old Pakistani, Arwin Bhus, walked through Cecil Court, near Leicester Square. He would always pause, fascinated, in front of the antique shop Louis Moyel. Sometimes he was accompanied by a young woman. She urged him to go on further, eager to look at the shop which was particularly fascinating for her: the antique jewellery shop Soldi.

She had already decided on her wedding present. This was the ring she wanted – no other would do. Arwin knew exactly which one she meant, but it would be a long time before they could get married. First of all he had to get a better job. Her parents were not keen; they were very doubtful about mixed marriages.

'Problems are bound to arise later, especially if you have children. You'll have problems which you just can't imagine now', they repeated over and over again. Arwin did not have this difficulty; he was an orphan and had been brought up by an uncle here in London. Eileen worked in the same office as him, though in a different department.

She was not especially interested in the other small shops in Cecil Court. Neither the world famous stamp collecting shop nor the one which only sold old mirrors and walking sticks with silver handles, nor the one with music hall programmes from the eighteenth and nineteenth centuries. Only two shops were of any interest to her: the antique jewellery shop and that which was to decide Arwin's future – at which one could only buy daggers, swords and sabres from all possible cultures from across several centuries.

His uncle also owned a small collection of these antique weapons. But none could be compared to this ceremonial sword, dating from the thirteenth century.

He would so love to own it. Of course, the price was very high. Perhaps he should go into the shop, just once, and see what happened.

He finally made the decision on a beautiful, warm spring day. His fiancée was not there. Perhaps that is why he had more courage and an urge to succumb to his desire which he could not explain even to himself. He entered the shop; apart from him the only other person present was a woman, maybe in her late fifties, who had worked there for many years.

"I'd like to have a look at that sword in the glass cabinet up there." The woman fetched a little ladder and took the sword down from the top shelf. She handed it to him and named a fairly high price. "One moment, please," she said "I just have to look it up in a book to tell you its exact history. Do you need it for the stage – I mean, the theatre – or for a museum? Or are you just a collector?"

Arwin could not reply; it was as if he had suddenly lost the power of speech. At last he was holding the sword. He needed no historical explanations – with this sword in his hands it was as if he were bewitched.

He felt as though he was a person from the thirteenth century and the sword was forcing him to act.

Elsie Beaton, the trustworthy saleswoman who had been employed at this shop for many years, became the victim of Arwin Bhus, a mad Pakistani. It was reported in The Times of London on March 2nd 1961.

When Arwin was interrogated by the police and later in court, he could not explain how it had happened.

"It must have been the sword, the ancient ceremonial sword," he said.

His fiancée was so upset that, in her agitation, she went and quickly bought the ring for herself from the other antique shop – and afterwards never returned to Cecil Court.

Benson

(For Erich Fried, to whom I once told the story of this journey
and who encouraged me to write it down.)

One of the TV programmes in England which my thir-
teen-year-old daughter had been watching with pleasure
here in London for two years was the American series,
'Benson'. She never failed to put it on, both Friday and Sunday
evenings. Benson, who could solve every problem in the end, who
had a witty answer to everything and who especially liked Katie,
the daughter of the house. 'Benson' was typically American, basi-
cally a harmless story which invariably had a happy ending. The
programme was very popular among teenagers.

It was through stories such as 'Benson' that my daughter
became attracted to America. She had a vague desire to watch this
programme one day in America itself, on a colour television – our
old-fashioned one was only black and white.

This was not the reason that the invitation from America was
so opportune. In America one speaks the same language as that
with which she was growing up. The mother, who had a different
native tongue, was also pleased about the invitation. The child
would probably feel at home there straightaway. Language was
so important, after all, whether one admitted it or not. Parents
of the same nationality, bringing up children in a second or third

different country but in their own language, were better off than parents of mixed nationalities who spoke to their children in the language of the country where they were living.

So they both welcomed the invitation from their second cousin. Emmy had been a widow now for almost two years, was a bit lonely, and was getting on in years. They shouldn't put off this journey for too long if they wanted to get to know an English speaking, American relation. She had been born in the small town of Mayen, near Koblenz, famous for Genoveva Castle which is said to have been built around 1280. As a teenager in the mid-twenties, Emmy had left with her parents for America.

Like so many others in those days, they emigrated simply in order to make a better life for themselves. Her grandmother and Emmy's mother had been sisters. Their children got on well together and had been writing to one another all their lives. And they visited each other every now and then.

So now in April, at Easter, the mother and daughter took a direct flight to Miami with Air Florida. Whilst landing they noticed a sign in the air: 'Welcome to Miami International Airport'. They had often seen this sign in thrillers on television at home.

The taxi driver was Columbian and of course spoke Spanish. All the street names were written both in English and Spanish – similar to Wales, where everything is in English and Welsh, a language which consists mainly of consonants. The taxi drove for nearly an hour under the sunny blue sky, down endless streets lined with palm trees on either side.

At last they came to the north district of the city. Now the taxi drove more slowly and at the end of 97th Street, it stopped. No. 387 was a large yellowish coloured building, surrounded by a park with lots of palm trees and two swimming pools in the distance at the back of the park. The entrance resembled a small border control. There was a yellow and black striped barrier which was only raised after the security guards, who were sitting in their little hut, had done their checks.

"Aha, you want to see Mrs. Strauss – are you the visitors from London?" He immediately used the house telephone to report the arrival of the visitors. "She's coming down right away."

I paid the waiting driver twenty five dollars for the 'short journey'. Somebody helped us carry the suitcases and we walked about fifty metres to the elegant doorway.

After a few minutes we heard the lift doors open and a small, elderly but heavily made-up woman came towards us, leaning on the arm of another old lady. This was the first time in her life that she had ever seen her second cousin Emmy. She would have liked to have been very emotional at this moment but all she felt was curiosity. Emmy introduced her friend to them, and they were helped into the lift with all their luggage. They went up to the fourth floor and walked along a veranda to the apartment. Looking down, they could see a large patio with tall, narrow palm trees which grew as high as the fourth floor. It was very hot and the sky was intensely blue. After twelve years in England, one could hardly believe that such wonderful warmth was the normal climate there. How stupid to have travelled carrying winter coats over their arms.

Now the door of Apartment No. 321 in Building A was unlocked. The flat had a light green carpet and a small lobby. On the right was a room with a sofa bed, wall-to- wall shelving and a door opening out on to a little balcony. On the left was a shower room. Then came the kitchen with a large fridge-freezer stocked with enough frozen milk, butter and bread to last for three months and a dishwasher which took hours to wash one plate.

Naturally, there was over-fierce air conditioning and three televisions, respectively in the kitchen, living room, and bedroom. Beautiful red roses (but made of porcelain) stood permanently on a table. Genuine Käthe Kruse dolls sat proudly on the chest of drawers. Otherwise there were the usual hand-crocheted little tablecloths, a comfortable sofa and an armchair upholstered in flowery material. In the glass cabinet were ornaments made of silver and porcelain. On the wall was an etching of the famous view of Heidelberg castle with the old bridge. The room was decorated in that particular bourgeois style common to all countries. Over the bed in their room hung a sort of heart-shaped wreath of roses, plastic of course. A present from Emmy's husband for St. Valentine's Day, which they had continued to celebrate even in their old age.

We sat down opposite one another in the first room with the sofa bed. "This is your bedroom," she told us. One could pull out the bed. The room did not have a door. She made a bit of space for our clothes in a cupboard already containing an iron, an ironing board and a linen basket. Then she asked: "Did you eat on the aeroplane?" and before we could reply, added: "Then you can't be hungry. I'll go down and eat now. Everyone eats supper very early here, at half past five. The food is excellent." And with that, she left.

Joanna began to cry. I, the mother, would have loved to have rung up the Argentine man to whom we had sub-let the flat in London and said to him: "Don't even unpack your things, we'll be back soon, our journey here was a mistake." For that was immediately clear. We went out onto the balcony and saw the two swimming pools and the American jacuzzi in the garden.

Comfortable, luxurious sunbeds were spread out under a wide straw shelter. We were both comforted by this sight.

Later on, during the first night, Cousin Emmy fell out of bed. Nurses and night staff appeared. Suddenly she said: "I helped immigrants a lot in the forties. Mrs. Eleanor Roosevelt acknowledged me in public for it. What sort of visa did you travel with, actually?" And then, in English to the night nurse: "Perhaps I'm living in the past, like lots of others here."

The house in which she lived was one of those typical American places where elderly, wealthy people live out their last years. A large sign at the entrance proclaimed the slogan: 'Add some years to your 70th, 80th, 90th'. One could rent expensive unfurnished flats there and bring one's own furniture, thus immediately feeling both at home and privileged. Medical supervision and night care was included in the price. So one paid handsomely not to be lonely and to have company of a similar age. Emmy's husband had been a stockbroker. That was the only thing in which she still actively took part. Every morning at eleven she listened to the New York stock market reports and studied in detail the complicated part of the 'Miami Herald' which was delivered each morning in its transparent plastic cover. If she was pleased with the news she would say "Oh, it went up". Although she was now over seventy years old, she wished to live for a long time still. So she bought and sold shares on the stock market whenever it seemed advantageous. Every day, she received the most complicated letters in the post. She seemed to follow all this perfectly, even though generally one did not know where one stood with her, as she kept changing her mind. She did not have any children. This house was inhabited exclusively by very smart elderly ladies and gentlemen, including rich Cubans who had turned their backs on Cuba after Castro came into power, and old ladies from Atlantic City and all sorts of other American cities and states. There were many emigrants from Europe, mainly German – often the first generation to be born in America. These elderly people had no lack of luxurious clothing in all possible colours. Despite their age, the ladies all had red varnished fingernails and smart hairdos. One of the youngest among them, who was still able to drive, showed us the beaches of Key Biscayne, Miami Beach etc. They were magnificent beaches with fine white sand. We also visited a zoo with many flamingos. We felt empowered by the feeling of summer. The nights under the star-filled skies were mild, with a constant chirping of crickets in the background. We felt good, we were in the tropics; it was beautiful.

We had accepted this invitation for two weeks. That was the arrangement. But suddenly on the fourth or fifth day, out of the blue, Cousin Emmy told us at breakfast that we could not stay with her any longer. She had some visitors arriving who wanted to stay the night with her. When her companion came round later, she tried to persuade her otherwise. With a pill in her hand she said, smiling: "Emmy, you can't do that. You already have visitors."

"Ring the airport and get them a flight home," Emmy insisted.

"I booked the flight for the end of next week and I let our flat in the meantime to help pay for travel costs," I said "but I'll see what I can do!"

I rang London and explained to the young man that we would have to return earlier than planned. He was very upset and said that he had to sit three exams before the end of April. "Please wait for a bit at least...otherwise it won't have been worth the long journey."

The next morning he rang back and said that he had not been able to sleep the whole night. "You know how small your flat is."

"I'll try to stay here longer," I answered. We spoke Spanish on the phone. Cousin Emmy was surprised: what was all this about , this Spanish and talk of London?

"The young man is Argentine; you know that I used to live in Argentina."

She did not quite believe me and became suspicious. Also, she said, in the dining-room downstairs last night there had been a conversation about the fact that I was a sympathiser of El Salvador and Nicaragua. In God's name, what sort of people had she invited to this house?

Now it was Friday and tomorrow was the first weekend after Easter; with the best will in the world there were no flights to be had until the next week. All one could do was to drive to the airport and hang around there until our names came up on a waiting list.

"You'll have to be patient until at least the middle of next week. We won't eat anything here, only sleep here."

"No, I've decided that tomorrow we'll drive to the airport with Mrs. Roberts." (Her companion, who was proud of having sat next to Ronald Reagan in the same class at school).

"We'll stay there until we've found something. There aren't any flights at the moment and we have to stay here at least until

Tuesday. We won't disturb you, we'll spend the whole day at the beach."

"No," she insisted, "that's impossible. And your telephone conversation in Spanish gave me food for thought." Now she came and stood very close to us. "I think I'll get you thrown out." And she left the apartment.

'Where's she going now?' I thought and followed her, taking her arm for a short distance down the corridor before I let go. 'She's probably going to a neighbour's now to chat a bit, or downstairs to be with the people who sit around in the hall in the evenings'.

It was eight o'clock and 'Benson' was due to be shown on the American TV. Joanna sat down on the comfortable sofa and turned on the colour television. She was looking forward to the programme. This time it was about revolutionaries visiting the 'Governor'. In the meantime I tried to ring a friend in California. I had just picked up the receiver when someone knocked on the door (there was no doorbell.) I asked my daughter to open it as I was still on the telephone. In came Jackie, the attendant from the dining-room and a man who was the equivalent of 'Maître d'Hotel'. The first thing Jackie did was to grab the receiver from my hand and hang it up.

Then the other man said: "You're leaving now." I could tell that there was no point in contradicting him. It was rather like a 'hold-up' or a raid in a gangster film. He immediately confiscated the transistor radio, the camera and Joanna's Swiss penknife, not letting us say a word.

"Is Mrs Emmy aware of what you're doing?"

"Oh yes."

"Tomorrow, when she notices what happened here, then ... "

He cut me off with the command: "Pack!"

Jackie sat down on the sitting room sofa. 'Benson' was still on. I fetched our suitcase and within ten minutes, everything was packed. We were pushed out of the back door. With great effort I managed to get our radio, camera and penknife back. He wanted to help us carry the suitcases downstairs but I said "Don't touch them!"

By the time we were on the street it was already dark. We had been constantly warned not to go outside after dark; the crime rate was very high. First of all we rang the doorbell of the house opposite. I asked if I could use their telephone to call a taxi. But they did not let us in. Then we dragged the suitcases to the main street. Cars raced past us. Of course no one could have any idea that we were in trouble. No sign of a taxi. So Joanna and I sat on our suitcases on the corner of 88th Street and another street which had a number in four figures. It seemed like an eternity. Opposite us an illuminated advertisement proclaimed the words: 'Add some years to your 70th, 80th, 90th'. We still could not quite take in what had happened or think what we could do to get away from here. Then suddenly, a bus appeared and stopped (although there was no bus stop). It was almost empty.

"We want to go to the airport," I said.

"Get in," said the driver and he helped us with our cases. "You can drive with me now to the terminal which is the last stop. From there you can get another bus all the way to the airport."

We drove for an hour in his bus and I wished that that hour would never come to an end. But then we arrived at a large bus station. There stood all the Greyhound buses which drive to all possible towns in America. From New Orleans and Mexico to Los Angeles. How stupid that I had not been able to contact the friend in California. We were so near and so far from everything.

A bus then drove us to the airport. There we put our suitcases in so-called 'lockers' and were put on the waiting list of Laker Airways. For three days and three nights we hung around at Miami Airport, sleeping on the floor. Hotels were simply too expensive. In the daytime we went to the beach, returning in the afternoons to see if we had had any luck in getting away. After three days and three nights, after Joanna had got terrible sunburn on her legs and we had had to look for a hospital and, as a result, could then produce a doctor's certificate, we were put on the 'priority list.' Altogether we had been in America for ten days.

At home again the following Friday evening, when we watched the Benson Show it just happened to be called 'Revolutionaries at the Airport', and once more it was a charming comedy with a happy ending.

In the end we were both not quite sure if we had really been to America or if it had just been another 'Benson Show.'

One or the Other

There was no lack of invitations and official receptions. She lived in exile. But the other one did not. It hardly worried her. If someone came from the other country she just greeted him or her with the words: "I'm the sister of ..." and she was immediately accepted.

That was her lifestyle.

"Do you happen to know ...?"

"Oh yes, she was at our place last Sunday."

"Of course, we know her well. She's coming for lunch next Sunday."

"And to us on Sunday week," added another voice.

Every now and then she telephoned the other one who was abroad and always had news to report.

But as the years went by she shrank a little; she had not been standing straight for a long time now and her skin had acquired a yellowish tinge. Every now and then she had fights with people whom she had known for years.

One day, the *Other One* came on an official visit. A large party was organised in her honour. She was surprised to see her suddenly here in the city in which she was living in exile.

Later, at the official reception, they happened to be standing next to one another. One of them had everything: fame, personality, family and no financial worries. All the other one had was the biological similarity of the TWIN SISTER.

Lord's Cricket Ground

Every May and June here at St John's Wood Underground Station, the escalators are checked over, the inside walls re-plastered and everything is prepared for the new cricket season at the so-called 'Lord's' opposite. And then people arrive, not only from towns all over England but also from all over the world, and the international cricket matches begin. When the game has ended, there are always traffic jams and then one sees that eighty per cent of the men in their red and yellow striped ties have come from Lord's, carrying those large, striped umbrellas. It usually rains a lot in June – also during the international tennis tournament at Wimbledon. That happens every year and one always hopes that next year it will be better.

The name Lord has nothing to do with God; it just happens to be the name of the founder. The ground is located in north London between Baker Street Station and Swiss Cottage Underground Station. The former is famous for the stories of Sir Arthur Conan Doyle (1859-1930) with those immortal characters Sherlock Holmes and Dr. Watson, who lived there at the (fictional) address which has now been made into a (real) museum. In between these two underground stations is St. John's Wood. It is a rather smart district and on the High Street there are very elegant shops, restaurants, and cafés with tables outside, weather allowing. This short, elegant little street could easily be in Brussels. Katherine Mansfield lived in this area nearly one hundred years ago, just off the High Street at 9, Acacia Road. A pear tree, mentioned in her stories, still stands in the front garden.

Opposite the stadium of Lord's Cricket Ground, where the international championships take place, is a small park which was once a graveyard. Grass grows between the old stones; on one side of the entrance is a little chapel and on the right hand side of the park is a playground. Many years ago, at the other side of the entrance, on Wellington Road, there used to be an art gallery called Lord's Art Gallery, which represented the artist Kurt Schwitters and housed a large collection of his paintings.

The first time I entered this park, I was very struck by the combination of graveyard and playground, having just come from a Catholic country. But after all, the graveyard had not been in use since the beginning of the century, and the children living in the middle of town needed somewhere to play. Otherwise they would have had to go to the playgrounds in Regents Park or Primrose Hill which were quite far away. And so, when my little daughter was still young and we came to this country in 1970, we too discovered this playground.

This park somehow felt right for me, for I had just come from the English Cemetery in Buenos Aires where the urn containing my mother's ashes had been buried. One could sit there for the whole afternoon. Sometimes a man came by with a thermos flask full of coffee, and sold me a cupful as though it were the most natural thing in the world.

The English Cemetery in Buenos Aires was next to the German Protestant one and the graves were simple. A bit further away was the monumental Catholic Cemetery, almost like a town. A friend, whose father was buried in the Catholic Cemetery was of the opinion that it was much more cheerful than the others, which were serious and lacking in any decoration. He was called Mario Bruto and was of Italian descent. However, his brother, who was a doctor, did not want to be called Dr. Bruto as he was afraid that he would not get enough patients. So he swapped two of the letters around and took on the English name of Burton.

A Meeting in the Park

When she took the child to school in the mornings and walked down the long corridor with all the books on display, it was the large flat ones with the titles such as 'This is Greece', 'This is Italy' or 'This is Spain' which caught her eye. She thought back to when, years ago when she was visiting this country, she had been given a book called 'This is London', not even dreaming in those days that she would one day be living here. 'But where is that book now?' she wondered.

One afternoon, after she had picked up the child from school, she wanted to go and buy a new recorder. The old one, imported from East Germany, which had been a present from the father of the child, had disappeared days ago and a replacement was needed. It was the end of June and a very hot summer's day. One of the child's classmates was allowed to come too. But first of all, they bought ice cream at Dinky's, the sweet shop in Chalbert St. opposite the school. Carrying their ice creams, they walked quite a long way through Regents Park and then took a taxi to the New London Music shop opposite the underground station at Great Portland St. The mother enjoyed going into a music shop again. She liked the atmosphere and it reminded her of earlier times. Of other music shops in other cities – for instance, Ricardi on Florida Street in Buenos Aires. Here, when one walked down the warm, summery street past the shop, classical music was usually floating out from within. It reminded her of Boosey and Hawkes in Berlin, Paris and London. Of the friend who worked in music and of the time when she herself had something to do with it. Of the music history lessons with Norbert Dufourcq and Roland Manuel, a friend of Ravel and Stravinsky at the Paris Conservatoire.

The mother bought each girl a tiny mouth organ, imported from Germany, and a book of music for beginners on the piano. When looking through it, she noticed that one of the pieces in it was called 'The Changing of the Guard.'

Now they walked back towards Regents Park. On the way, they bought three more ice creams. It was such a hot day that it dripped all over them and they had to lick up the drips more quickly.

They had just passed the newly erected statue of John Kennedy, when as if it were a warning, the mother's sunglasses fell off. The frame had snapped behind her left ear. Quickly they ran over to a side street filled with traffic and in the process, the mother's ice cream fell on to the ground. 'What a shame' she thought and comforted herself with the words: 'Oh well.'

Now they had reached the other side of the park again. They sat down on a bench to rest for a moment. The children took it in turns to play their recorder. The little friend could play 'God save the Queen' rather well. After a while, they went on through the park.

Every now and then, the children drank some water from the small, rectangular drinking fountains which are provided in the parks here, just like on the plazas in Buenos Aires. Another thing that the English have in common with the Argentines and Portuguese – as well as the same round red pillar boxes, around 1.70 metres in height. The mother started reminiscing about her first time in London again. About the first small collapsible pram which one could buy cheaply in a shop called Mothercare. It was exactly the same as the one which, in those days, had stood in front of a house in Blenheim Crescent – where she had again lived when she came back to this city after a gap of fifteen years – and from where she had been thrown out so outrageously. Now they were standing in front of a gate with vertical bars decorated in gold, leading into the rose garden; the other path continued through the flat park.

"Let's go this way," she said to the children, who were a few paces ahead of her. And suddenly she found herself staring into the face of a seven-year-old boy, sitting on a bicycle. He had blond curly hair (like that other boy, she thought) a strange, drooping mouth and blue eyes. The moment she identified him, she heard a woman's voice calling her name from behind the gate. She turned round and recognised her. The woman came up to her, beaming, as if she was pleased to see her, proving that the little boy was indeed her son. And so they went on together through the park – which had been a haven to her long ago, when forced by the other one to move out of the house so quickly. That is to say, she had been offered the basement flat in the same house, but she could not face the damp walls, and the dustbins as decorations in front of the main window and front door. During that time, in order to recover, she had returned again and again in the afternoons with her eighteen months old daughter to this beautiful, large park.

Years had gone by since then.

"How is your mother?" said one of them in German.

"My mother died two years ago".

"Oh, I'm sorry to hear that".

"Is that your daughter?" and she pointed to one of the girls.

"Yes, the one on the left is my daughter. The one on the right is a school friend. They're in the same class. Her mother is Swedish and the father is Indian. There are all sorts of mixtures here in this country. We've just been to buy a new recorder."'

"Do you play the recorder too?"

"No, unfortunately not."

"I do, and we've had a piano too for some time now."

"How lovely!"

Then one of them said that she had just seen the play

'Kennedy's Children' by Robert Patrick in the Arts Theatre and she had been very impressed by it.

"Oh, so was I," said the other. "I saw it four times. It's mainly about identification and monologues."

They had already reached the other side of the park. One of them looked at her watch. It was twenty to six. She had to hurry, for the girls had to be at the Girl Scouts by six. She held out her hand to say goodbye. However, the other ignored the hand, as though she were on guard and quickly said: "I'll ring you, I've got your number". But of course they both knew that neither of them would ever ring the other and they swiftly went their separate ways.

She was the one who had given her the book 'This is London'.

Clayton

In the first hotel on the left coming from the direction of the Passarelle on the Rue Saint-Louis-en-L'Ile, along with various other foreigners, lived a young Canadian called Clayton. This was from the middle to the end of the 1950s. Clayton was twenty-four years old; like so many other young men, he had come to Paris with great hopes and expectations. His father was a bishop in the English-speaking part of Canada and sometimes he would proudly tell people that his family had originally been Quakers who had emigrated to Canada more than 150 years ago. Apart from that, little was known about his past.

His father did not approve of his plans, so he earned the money for his journey to Paris by working as a car mechanic at a garage. And he earned so much money that he was able to live in Paris on these earnings for at least a year. At that time, the Canadian dollar was strong in comparison to the French franc.

He looked nice and harmless, was of medium height, had blonde hair, blue eyes and an impressive nose, and was friendly and attractive to women. He led a very spartan life, and had a heavy yet balanced gait rather like a sailor accustomed to walking on board ships. He liked to wear a velvet jacket. He was usually to be seen on the island with a large notebook under his arm and a thick pencil in his hand. In the same hotel lived George Arnaud, the French author who had written the novel 'Wages of Fear' which had been so successfully filmed by Henri-Georges Clouzot in 1952. Clayton often sat with Arnaud in the Alsace restaurant on the island named 'The Oasis', where one could get the best tomato salad, the best Frankfurters and the best sauerkraut in the world alongside a glass of beer. He was proud of his friendship with Arnaud and also liked to show off the postcards which he had received from Ezra Pound who was, in those days, in prison in America and was famous for his correspondence with many young unknown people.

In the summer he often drank his morning coffee at the café on the corner of the Rue des Deux Ponts. Chagall was also often to be seen at the same café because one of his daughters lived on the island. People admired the shape of Chagall's eyes, and he always wore a sort of worker's outfit in blue; perhaps it was an early model of blue jeans.

In a very beautiful flat, opposite this café, almost at the tip of the island, lived a Canadian woman of Irish descent. She was about twenty years older than Clayton and came from the part of Canada where he had lived. He was a sort of protégé of hers in the sense that she took him seriously, introduced him to already well-known artists and managed to get him a job at UNESCO – if only as a general dogsbody – where she herself worked, when his money began to run out.

One day a young American, the publisher of a literary journal in the USA, appeared on the island. He was staying in one of the hotels there and got to know Clayton, whom he liked and valued. The American was someone who liked discovering young talent, much as Ford Madox Ford had discovered Jean Rhys in the twenties, and had been the first to publish her short story 'Vienne' in his journal 'The Transatlantic Review.'

But Clayton did not want to show the American any of his work. The latter was patient and waited for a long time. He said he would dedicate half of his next journal to Clayton's work. But neither he nor anyone else got to see anything at all. The only thing Clayton gave him was a photo of himself sitting at a table with a single rose.

Thus Clayton's life went on for several years; he kept his head above water with various short term jobs and got into trouble with the police once, because he wanted to climb up the outside wall of Notre Dame.

The people who had been so important to him at the beginning of his stay in Paris no longer took him seriously.

He became rather lonely and got together after a while with a cabaret singer living in the neighbourhood. She already had three children by different men. Clayton gave her one more child, grew a beard and returned to Canada.

Of Traces and Names

From the start, the English summers were hard for me. One year we arrived here on April 27th and the ship left the harbour of Buenos Aires on April 10th. There it was already autumn and the trees were partly bare although it was still warm; lots of people were spending Easter at the seaside, at Mar del Plato or places like that, and could even still bathe in the sea. The Argentine cruise ship bore the impressive name of 'Libertad'. My little daughter was now thirteen months old and, since it was only children under one year who were allowed to travel free, we had to pay half the price of her passage. We took her cot with us and set it up in the cabin. Had she noticed that we were all of a sudden somewhere else? She was the most elegant baby on board and I was complimented on her over and over again.

Once, many years before, when I was on a visit to Buenos Aires once again, before I ever realized that I would one day end up living in England, I was at the house of Jorge Luis Borges. His mother was still alive and it was the flat in Maipu Street 994, on the top floor of a modern white building opposite the Plaza San Martin. I remember Borges commenting on the lift in his house and saying that often it did not work, which was problematic. Up there we drank tea or cocoa and ate some biscuits. He opened the conspicuous glass-fronted cabinet for me and took out the sword which had belonged to his grandfather, Colonel Francisco Borges.

Jorge Luis never mentioned of his own accord that he was blind. He only said: "no veo" or "es porque no veo" – because I can't see. He knew that I was called Edith and that I had emigrated from Germany to Argentina. That was sufficient introduction and he then said: "Please, take the book by Heine off the shelf, it's up there" (pointing to it) "and read 'The Battle of Hastings' aloud to me." Naturally he spoke German and, out of admiration for the author Kafka, had translated 'Die Verwandlung' (Metamorphosis) into Spanish. He also admired Gustav Meyring very much and told us about his book 'Der Golem'. He himself had also written a poem with the same title.

Naturally I had heard of the Bayeux Tapestry and about the Battle of Hastings and had, in Paris, left behind a book about them with reproductions.

In 1966 – the same year that my mother died – there was a lot written about the Battle of Hastings on its 900th anniversary. 'When I'm back in Europe' I thought to myself, 'I'll go to Hastings and also to Bayeux' – which I later did.

Some years later, when my daughter was older, I found some work in Germany during the summer months. That was always very nice and enabled me to refresh my language as well as finding my original roots again.

However, when summer arrived again and I had to stay in England this time, new problems arose. In the long run, one does feel diminished by exile; one has to feel at home somewhere, even if only in the language. So I tried to help myself by reading good literature, and the year before I had read 'Waltham Abbey'.

"Waltham Abbey? But I don't know anything about it. I don't know Waltham Abbey, I've never even heard the name."

"But I know for certain that the evening before I left, your papa said to me: 'Melusine is bound to know it; she knows everything and I believe she knows Waltham Abbey better than Treptow or Strelau.'"

"That's how reputations get made," laughed Melusine. "Papa just said that by chance, he was just looking for an example. And now look what's come of it! Never mind, tell me, what is Waltham Abbey? And where is it?"

"It's quite near London and one can visit it in just one afternoon, like going to the Mausoleum in Charlottenburg or the Friedenskirche in Potsdam."

"Is it a sort of mausoleum then?"

"Yes and no. There's no monument but the whole church is like a sort of monument."

"Monument to whom?"

"To King Harold."

"For the King Harold whom Edith Swan-Neck searches for on the battlefield of Hastings?"

"The very one."

"While I was in London I saw that picture by Horace Vernet of the moment when the beautiful Col de Cygne is wandering distractedly among the dead. I remember that there were two monks walking along beside her. But I can't remember any more. And I don't know at all what happened in the end."

"What happened – that's the last act of the drama and this last act is called Waltham Abbey. The monks, you remember, who were walking alongside Edith, were the monks of Waltham Abbey and when they at last found what they were looking for, they laid the king on thick tree branches and carried him all the way back to Waltham Abbey. And they buried him there."

"And did you visit his grave?"

"No, not his grave. That doesn't exist. All that is known is that they buried him there. And when I stood there at sunset in an ancient grove of lime trees, with gravestones either side and the evening church bells began to ring, it seemed to me as if the procession of the monks was approaching again and I saw Edith and also saw the King even though he was half covered with twigs. According to Fontane in 'Der Stechlin.'"

After I had read that, I put down the book, picked up the modern telephone, pressed the keys 192 and inquired about the telephone number for London Transport.

"How do I get from here" (I named the part of London where I lived) to Waltham Abbey?"

"Very easy" said the voice on the other end of the telephone. "Take the Underground, in your case the Central Line, to Loughton. From there you can catch the 250 Eastern National bus, through Epping Forest, and you'll be there in 35 minutes."

An hour and a half later I was standing in front of Waltham Abbey, the first Norman church to be built, 6 years before the Norman invasion in 1060. And that happened because Harold, the Earl of Wessex, and later the last Anglo-Saxon King of England, wanted to have a beautiful church built in Waltham. He got his masons to come from France because they were famous for their good solid buildings with high vaulting and round arches, thick pillars, massive walls, and the square towers. After the conquest of England, Norman or Romanesque churches or castles were built throughout the country.

Now, I stood in front of Waltham Abbey and did not at first know why it made me think of Husum. I had been there on a similar pilgrimage once upon a time.

It was a normal weekday and there was no lack of tourists. This church had been a place for pilgrims and worshippers for nearly a thousand years. At first, the holy cross of Waltham, which worked miracles and cured the sick, was kept here. There were so many wonderful stories up to the year 1540. Tovi the Proud had brought the 'Holy Cross' here around 1030 and built the first small church.

If one stands in the middle of the church, one sees a large embroidered and painted wall-hanging on the left at the back, on which King Harold is depicted. At the top is written his name and that he was the founder of this church. I wanted to know more, and saw that the other tourists were holding little booklets, like Baedekers, and were now better informed.

"Can one buy that?" I asked someone standing next to me.

"Yes, over there." said someone else immediately, pointing.

I had already noticed a priest walking up and down the aisles.

Actually, I should ask him, I thought, and followed him down a few steps to a small room and a sort of shop. I asked him which book he would recommend. He showed me some and told me their prices. He had a very strong foreign accent which surprised me, not Scottish, Welsh, or Irish. After a short conversation, I dared to ask him where he came from "Oh I'm German," he said. "I've been here for 47 years – I stayed on after the war." I wondered if he had been a prisoner of war but did not say anything.

"I lived out here in Waltham Cross and always came to this church, so I belonged to the Waltham community and got this job. Because the miserable old-age pension doesn't cover very much."

"So you're not a vicar or a priest?" I asked without meaning to.

"Oh no, I only wear this black habit for work."

"And where do you come from in Germany if I may ask?"

"From Berlin, East Berlin. I was there last month; my brother still lives there."

Then I showed him the text about Waltham Abbey in the book by Fontane which I had with me, but he had never heard of it.

"What is your profession?"

"Car mechanic," he said, and at once added "King Harold's grave is outside in the garden. On the ground is a big square stone and his name is chiselled on it. It's assumed that his remains were buried there. And you'll find his statue in the southwest porch."

I go out straight away and see the stone.

It is a wonderful, sunny, late afternoon in July 1990. I walk around a bit in the little park. On the right-hand side are more graves, but I do not approach them. I see a little open-air café on a terrace directly opposite the church. Several tables and chairs are still free, and tourists are sitting there having afternoon tea. I sit down at a table too, order a cup of tea or cocoa, and choose a piece of cake. I'm happy to have come here so spontaneously and feel good. Then I see someone in a black robe, coming over the shining green lawn towards me. He is waving a small light blue booklet in his hand, entitled 'The Legend of the Miraculous Cross of Waltham'. Joyfully beaming, he gives it to me saying in

German: "I was interested after all. All the stories are in here." He does not want any money for it. I leaf through it, and discover that Harold was the son of the powerful Jarl Godwine and the brother of the wife of King Edward the Confessor. She was called Edith too. After the death of King Edward, Harold the Second was crowned as the next king. He came back from the battle of Stamford Bridge and prayed here in Waltham before fighting William of Normandy in the battle of Hastings.

Osgod and Ailric, the two monks in the painting by Horace Vernet, watched from the distance while King Harold fell in the battle of Hastings. He got shot in the eye by an arrow. If one examines the Bayeux Tapestry closely, one can see this in the far right corner. The two monks, Osgod and Ailric, begged William of Normandy for permission to bury King Harold in Waltham. Apparently William was touched by that and gave them permission, refusing to accept the money they had offered him. And so Osgod and Ailric searched for their King; they could not find him among the mutilated corpses, however, and had to go home without having completed their task.

This is what Heine writes in his 'Battlefield at Hastings':

Asgod and Ailric so they spake;
His hands the Abbot clasped,
Down sat, despairing, sunk in thought,
Then sighed and said at last:
At Grendelfield, near Bardenstone,
In the wood's deepest dell,
Lone in a lonely pauper-cot
Doth swan-necked Edith dwell.
'Swan-necked', men named her – for
Her neck, of smoothest pearl,
Was swan-like arched – Harold the King,
He loved the comely girl.
Her hath he loved and cherished and kissed
But later on, abandoned and forgot;
The years roll by – full sixteen years

The False Houses

Have watched her widowed lot.
Brothers, to her betake yourselves,
And with her back return
To Hastings field; this woman's glance
Will there the king discern.

And further on in the same poem:

The whole drear day had watched her search,
The stars still see her seek;
All of a sudden from the woman's lips
Breaks shrill a dreadful shriek:
Edith had found the royal corpse!
No longer need she seek;
No word she spake, she wept no tear,
She kissed the pale, pale cheek.
She kissed the brow, she kissed the lips,
Her arms about him pressed,
She kissed the deep wound blood-besmeared
Upon her monarch's breast.
And at the shoulder looked she too
And them she kissed contented
Three little scars, joy-wounds her love in
Passion's hour indented.
Meanwhile the Monks from out the wood
Some twisted branches bring;
This was the leafy bier whereon
They laid their slaughtered king.
To Waltham Abbey they did go
For there to bury him;
And her beloved's corpse
Did Edith Swan-Neck follow.

Heinrich Heine tells us of the French source of his poem: Augustin Thiery, Histoire de la Conquête d'Angleterre par les Normandes. 1838.

There are further reports of a crippled beggar woman named Edith Crikel, who is said to have approached the altar in Waltham on two crutches, taken a coin from there, and hidden it under her tongue. As she hobbled down from the third step, her body arched from the kidneys upwards. Antonius, the churchwarden in those days, slapped her three times hard on the back and she began to cough, and spat out a lump of blood as big as an apple. Inside it was the coin. The woman owned up to the theft but stayed deformed for the rest of her life.

Someone else had stolen silver and gold and artefacts from the church and wanted to sell them to a goldsmith named Theodonic on the way to London. But it turned out that he was the very man who had made them for Waltham in the first place.

This all happened during the time when the miraculous holy cross was still at Waltham. Geoffrey of Mandeville, who later became the Earl of Wessex, wanted to destroy Waltham and remove the cross from its place, but was then fatally wounded during the storming and siege of Burwell in 1144. And there were more and more legends about this cross of Waltham. Then in 1540, the church was partly abandoned.

As one can read in history books, even Henry the Eighth had an affection for Waltham and intended to build a cathedral there, but it never happened. The restoration of the church did not start until 1859 and Fontane probably visited it during his travels to London between 1844 and 1859.

Now, to finish this story, I have to describe a second summer outing.

A second visit to Mont Saint Michel in Normandy, after a gap of twelve years. One can only visit this fort, church, and cathedral all in one, with a guide. Our group was led by a young Frenchman who spoke very good English. As we entered a wonderful bare room which was used as a church over a thousand years ago and was the cradle of Gregorian chant, he casually mentioned that it had been historically proven that William of Normandy came here to pray before setting off for the Battle of Hastings.

The Flower Seller on the Corner of the Rue d'Alésia

When she was first offered the room in this district, she did not have a particularly good feeling about it. Although she was not that interested in the past any more – twelve years had passed by now – this area still reminded her of that particular period of her life. There was the Rue d'Alésia with its acacia trees. She had often ridden her bicycle up and down it. Just two minutes by foot from the Métro station Plaisance was the Rue Raymond Losserand; her first flat in Paris had been on the corner of that street and the Rue Ridder. Perhaps not exactly a flat – just a room, which in those days cost 6,000 old French francs per month, including the use of the kitchen and a bathroom. Naturally there was hot water and heating and even a small balcony with a view over the green lawns of the Hôpital Laennec, where sometimes there was even a little sheep to be seen.

The loo had been clean enough and had a seat. The importance of this did not occur to her until she lived in this primitive 'chambre de bonne' in the district which was for her both old and new.

She had not been able to find anything better and was obliged to live temporarily in this room. In the meantime, prices had gone up to one hundred new Francs a month, not including charges for water – though in the corridor there was a washbasin where the tenants of the sixth floor met with their jugs, like people from the Middle Ages meeting by a well. The difference being that wells are beautiful whereas it was better not to inspect this washbasin too closely. The heating consisted of a portable Calor gas stove which seldom worked. She arranged everything in the room as well as she could but nevertheless it was only with great effort that she could feel even just a bit at home there.

She had never imagined that one day her daily evening walks would include a search for a halfway decent café or restaurant where she could take advantage of a clean loo. She often went to Brasserie Zeyer on the corner of the Avenue du Maine expressly for this purpose.

Twelve years ago, he had lived directly opposite, at 91 Rue d'Alésia on the fifth floor, and even now the flower seller still had her stall in front of the Brasserie – although the latter did not recognise her any more. The flower seller was the only witness left from that time. He had often cycled with her down the Avenue d'Orléans, which was lined with acacia trees. They had also often visited the nearby Cinéma Montrouge on the corner of the Rue d'Alésia where now, in 1964, they were showing 'La Soupe aux Beurres' starring Fernandel and Bouvril in the main roles. Being a highly intellectual person, he never knew what to do with her. He kept resorting to the cinema and he could not even talk about the films properly with her. Of course she was a nice, pretty girl. But as the date of arrival of his girlfriend from the other part of the world approached, he took her to the cinema more and more.

It was she who had found the room for him on the corner of the Rue d'Alésia. At the Alliance Française on the Boulevard Raspail there was a noticeboard displaying advertisements for rooms to let. This room was actually quite cheap, had a desk and a comfortable armchair, only at certain times of the day the noise blaring up from the street was quite disturbing – but after all, one could not have everything.

Shortly before Christmas, his previous girlfriend from the other part of the world arrived in Paris. He immediately explained that he could not leave Francisca alone at Christmas; she did not know anyone here and, anyway, she had only come to Paris in order to see him. And perhaps it would be best not to meet for a week. In the meantime he would come to a decision and then they could celebrate New Year together.

"Alright," she said, "I'll go and see my father. He's always alone at Christmas and he's bound to be pleased."

When she got back to Paris, there was a message from him waiting for her. She had had a terrible week which seemed never-ending. Hesitantly, she opened the letter. He had written that he still could not decide but anyway they could not see each other on New Year's Eve. Everything would become clearer after the holidays.

She ran to the telephone and rang up a girlfriend. 'Just keep going' she kept repeating to herself: 'Keep going.' The friend was free and thought it a good idea to spend the evening together. They went for a walk along the banks of the Seine and around Nôtre Dame. They were both excited by the novelty of Paris. It was a wonderfully clear and starry night and not all that cold for the time of year. The down-and-outs had gathered just opposite Nôtre Dame, on the riverbank. They were passing a bottle, or rather, several bottles around, and a Christmas tree was propped against a lamp post. They appeared to be happy. Perhaps he too would go for a walk somewhere with the other one, she thought. Midnight was approaching. A special bell, used only for this particular ceremony, was ringing. It sounded dark, slow and distant. Was it still Quasimodo who rang the bell? Everyone was calling 'Bonne Année!' to one another, car horns were being hooted: it was New Year. The girls embraced.

"Don't take it so seriously," said the friend.

"It's not the first time – let's see what happens!"

On the Place de St Michel was a kiosk selling chocolates. She quickly bought two big boxes and gave one to her friend. A taxi drew up; someone got out, they climbed in and drove away. Her friend got out at the Rue de l'Observatoire, where she was living at the time in an international student hostel.

"Come to lunch with me tomorrow at twelve." she said. The two girls hugged, then, the box of chocolates tucked under her arm, the friend did her best to comfort her, patting her shoulder and looking at her sympathetically. "See you tomorrow!"

She waited until the friend was safely inside the hostel. Then she said to the chauffeur: "Now to the Rue Raymond Losserand." He drove down the Avenue Général Leclerque. Soon they came to the church with the tall steeple on the corner of the Rue d'Alésia. It was brightly lit up, inside and out; probably a midnight mass. There stood the flower seller, even at this late hour.

"Please stop for a moment," she said to the driver. Quickly she got out of the taxi and gave the other box of chocolates to the flower seller. Staring at her, her mouth open in surprise, the woman took the chocolates, then straightaway understood. She saw the tears running down the girl's cheeks. She embraced her and gave her all the roses she had left.

"Don't treat it too much like a tragedy," she said. But they both could not help glancing up at the window on the third floor. It was brightly illuminated and behind the thin curtain two shadows were silhouetted.

"Senora, Feliz Año Nuevo," said the girl. "Y gracias por las rosas." And she quickly shut the taxi door so that the chauffeur could drive on.

'What a New Year' she thought to herself, and her salty tears fell onto the roses.

I would like to thank several people for their role in bringing this book, my first publication in English, to fruition.

First, I appreciate deeply the work of the two translators, Rachel Isserlis and Barbara Lester. The translation into English was originally the idea of Steven Isserlis, who also read the proof. And finally I would like to thank my daughter Joanna Bergin, whose support has been invaluable - as it has been in so many areas of my life.